THE GUNSMITH

454

Into the Fire

Books by J.R. Roberts
(Robert J. Randisi)

The Gunsmith series

Lady Gunsmith series

Angel Eyes series

Tracker series

Mountain Jack Pike series

COMING SOON!

The Gunsmith
455 – Brotherly Love

For more information visit:
www.SpeakingVolumes.us

THE GUNSMITH

454

Into the Fire

J.R. Roberts

SPEAKING VOLUMES, LLC
NAPLES, FLORIDA
2019

Into the Fire

ISBN 978-1-64540-165-0

Chapter One

Clint Adams was a good cook.

He was wearing an apron and standing in front of a stove that had several steaks in various pans going. The apron was tied so that it wouldn't inhibit his motion if he had to grab for his gun. But he didn't expect to have to do that while in the kitchen of the Well Done Café.

"Those steaks ready, yet?" Denise Parker asked, rushing into the kitchen.

"Coming up," Clint said.

He used a large fork to spear all three steaks and drop them onto a plate, then smothered them in onions and vegetables.

"Ready to go!" he called out.

Denise picked up all of the plates and expertly balanced them on her arms.

"Get three more goin'," she said, over her shoulder. "Word's gettin' around town that we've got the best steaks—thanks to you."

When he first rode into Tenafly, Montana he never expected to be working with an apron on . . .

***

Clint liked Montana in the Fall. The air was crisp, and Eclipse's ears always perked up. When he rode into Tenafly, he was ready for a good bed, steak and beer. Eclipse was ready for a thorough rubdown.

He got the horse settled, then found his way to the Hotel Benedict. Once he dropped off his rifle and saddle-bags in his room, he hit Main Street and started looking to satisfy his needs.

A beer came first at a saloon called The Whiskey River—not particularly original, but accurate, since rivers of whiskey did flow in most saloons, along with maybe oceans of beer.

"Beer," he said to the bartender.

"Comin' up."

When the bartender served it, Clint asked, "And when I'm done here, could you point me toward a good meal?"

"No problem," the man said. "Just tell me when."

Clint didn't nurse the beer. He drained it fairly quickly and then waved at the bartender.

"Down the street about two blocks is a café called the Well Done," the man said. "It's owned by a woman named Denise. You'll get a good meal, there."

"Thanks."

"Then get on back here for more beer."

"Got it."

Clint left the Whiskey River and headed for the Well Done . . .

***

The café was medium-sized, with plenty of available tables, particularly ones in the back. Most social diners preferred to sit near a window, or in the center of the room.

The woman who greeted him might've been Denise, he couldn't be sure. Since Denise was the owner, she may have been in the kitchen. This woman was an attractive blonde in her mid-thirties.

"A back table?" she repeated. "Take any one you want."

"Thank you."

He went to a table while she went to the kitchen. She came out balancing plates up and down her arms, set them down on a table where a family of four was seated.

That done, she hurried over to Clint's table—a bit frantically, he thought.

"What can I get you?" she asked.

"Would a steak be too much trouble?" he asked. "You seem . . . busy."

"I lost my cook, so I'm doin' both, cookin' and servin'," she said.

"Well, I'm not in a hurry," he said. "I'll make do with some coffee while you prepare the steak, when you have a chance."

"Thank you," she said, "but you'll get your food as quickly as all these others."

She turned and hurried back to the kitchen. When she returned, she served two more tables before running back to the kitchen. He was starting to wish he'd gone somewhere else and not added to her burden.

When she reappeared, she brought him his coffee. He watched as she served three more tables before bringing him his steak. He was hungry, and it took care of that, but he'd had better.

While he was eating, each of the other tables finished their meals and left. By the time he was done, he was the only customer left.

The woman, seeming noticeably more relaxed, came to his table.

"You look like you finally got to take a deep breath," he said.

"I did," she said. "I'm sorry, you came in at a busy time."

"Will you be able to hire another cook?" he asked.

"Probably not."

"Why?"

She sat across from him.

"You just got to town, right? Then you don't know what's been goin' on," she said. "Someone's been tryin' to run me out of business."

"How?"

"They've beaten up three of my cooks, forcin' them to quit," she said. "Then they sabotaged some of my supplies, saltin' my meats."

"Have you gone to the law?"

"The Sheriff says he really hasn't been able to find out anythin'," she said.

"Do you think he's been trying?"

"Well," she said, "he's not a very good lawman."

Clint ate his last piece of steak and pushed the plate away."

"Anythin' else?" she asked.

"Pie?"

"Apple, or peach?"

"Oh, peach," he said. "Always peach."

"And coffee?"

"Please."

She stood and said, "Comin' up."

Chapter Two

Clint left the Well Done after enjoying the peach pie more than the steak. He hoped Denise would be able to find herself another cook, one who could do a steak properly.

He decided to walk off the meal and enjoy the crisp night Montana air. The town was a decent size, large enough to have more than one saloon, hotel, and several restaurants. He stopped into a saloon to have another beer. It was a busy place, larger than the Whiskey River, called the Montana Grand. The bar was twice as long as the one in the Whisky, and it had several gaming tables, as well as a wheel of fortune. In addition, there were four girls circulating on the floor.

He saw that two of the gaming tables were poker, and the third faro. At the moment, though, none of them attracted him as much as the bar did.

"Beer," he said to the bartender.

The man nodded and set the brew in front of him, then went back to his busy bar.

Clint picked up the beer, then turned to further examine the room while he sipped. The crowd was loud, but orderly, which was sort of unusual in an establishment like the Grand. Where men gathered there was usually an argument going on somewhere.

Clint finished his beer, turned to set the empty mug down on the bar.

"Another?" the bartender asked.

"Sure." When the man set the second beer down Clint said, "And some information."

"What kind of information?"

"Restaurants here in town," Clint said. "How are they?"

"The Woodbury Steakhouse is very good, the Lakewood Café is okay, probably better for breakfast than supper. Oh, what hotel are you in?"

"The Benedict."

"Oh yeah, the Benedict's dining room ain't bad."

"Is that it?"

The man shrugged.

"I passed another one on the street called the Well Done," Clint said. "You didn't mention that one."

"Well, that one's owned by Denise Parker."

"And?"

"She's . . . not popular in this town."

"Why's that?"

The bartender looked down the bar and then said, "Excuse me, more customers."

Clint picked up his second beer and took a drink.

"I couldn't help hearin' you fellas talkin'," the man next to him said.

Clint looked at him. He was a short, middle-aged man with a grey-streaked black beard. In front of him was a mug with remnants of a beer in it.

"Kind of hard not to hear conversations in a saloon," Clint said.

"You know it," the man commented. "You lookin' for a place to eat?"

"I'm always interested in a good steak. You got some advice about where to go?"

The man picked up his empty mug and looked into it.

"Another beer?" Clint asked.

"Thanks," the man said, putting the mug down.

Clint waved to the bartender.

"Give my friend a fresh beer."

The bartender put it down in front of the smaller man. "Made yourself a new friend, Eddie?"

As the barman moved off, Clint said, "Eddie?"

"Eddie Mason, at your service."

"Tell me about restaurants," Clint said.

Chapter Three

"I actually like the Well Done," Eddie Mason said. "Or, I did two cooks ago."

"What's going on, Eddie?" Clint asked. "Who's got it in for Denise?"

"I don't know who, exactly," Eddie said. "I know a lot of the town seems to."

"Why is that?"

"Well," Eddie said, "if I had to guess . . ."

"That's what I'm asking you to do."

"Well, she came to town a while ago and opened her café," Eddie said. "We already had the Woodbury and the Lakewood. I don't think people liked having a stranger open a new place."

"Could it be one of those owners who's got it in for her?"

"Maybe," Eddie said. He finished his beer, then looked into his glass. "I might know more if I wasn't so thirsty."

"Why do I get the feeling," Clint said, "that I already know all you know."

The bartender came over and looked at Clint, who shook his head.

"You're done, Eddie," the man said. "Out."

With a mournful look on his face, Eddie slunk out of the saloon.

"What did he tell you?" the bartender asked.

"His opinion, I guess," he said. "How soon after Denise opened the Well Done did her troubles start?"

"I think you better ask her," the bartender said.

"Not my business, really," Clint said.

"Another beer?"

"No, thanks. I'll just finish this one."

The man nodded and moved on down the bar.

Another man sidled up next to Clint, this one thin and in need of a shave and a bath.

"Buy me a beer and I'll tell ya a few things," the man said.

Clint had half his beer left, so he pushed it over to the man and said, "Finish this one. I've got to go."

He left without looking back, but swore he could hear the man guzzling the beer.

***

In the morning he decided to go to the Lakewood Café for breakfast. It was busy, but he managed to wrangle a back table. He noticed that the place was furnished more expensively than the Well Done. There were two men and a woman waiting tables. One of the men came over to him.

"Do you need to see a menu, sir?"

"No," Clint said, "I'll have bacon-and-eggs, and some biscuits, please."

"And to drink?"

"Coffee."

"Right away."

The waiter went across the room and through a door, which probably led to the kitchen. The other waiter then came out the same door, carrying plates.

Clint could see that the place was significantly more successful than the Well Done. Why then would the owner try to force Denise Parker out of business? It didn't make a lot of sense.

He noticed, while he ate, that the waitress kept looking over at him. She appeared to be in her late twenties, tall, slender, brunette. It became very obvious that she was interested in him. She even bumped into one of the waiters while staring over.

When he finished eating, he paid his bill and started for the door, but the way was blocked by the waitress.

"I think I know you," she said.

"Do you?"

"I think so," she said, "but I can't be sure." Up close she was even prettier than he thought.

"Then how would we make sure?" he asked.

"Meet me," she said, "after work."

"When do you finish here?" he asked.

"At three," she said.

"What's your name?"

"Laura."

"I'll come by at three, Laura," he said.

"Good."

"Do you want to know my name?" he asked.

"No," she said, "I want to see if I can remember on my own. You can tell me at three. I have to go back to work, now."

She stepped aside and allowed him to leave the café.

***

Once again he walked around town, attracting glances from people on the street—admiring from women, curious from men. Eventually, he found himself across from the Woodbury Steakhouse. It had the name painted ornately across large, plate glass windows on either side of the front door. You could see practically every diner at their table through those windows.

It didn't seem the kind of place he'd ever be able to comfortably have a meal.

Chapter Four

He thought about Laura, from the Lakewood, for the rest of the afternoon 'til three. He couldn't remember ever having met her before.

Waiting outside the café for her to appear, he wondered if she would remember where she'd seen him before. Or if that had just been a way to get him to come back?

When she finally came out and saw him standing there she smiled. Without her apron she looked even trimmer.

"You're here!" she said.

"Didn't you think I'd come back?"

"I wasn't sure."

"Is that why you told me you thought you knew me?" he asked. "To get me to come back."

"Well . . ."

"We don't know each other, do we?" he asked.

She averted her eyes before answering.

"Well," she said, "if you walk me home, by the time we get there we'll know each other."

"All right," he said. "I'll go that far."

They started to walk.

"When did you arrive in town?" she asked.

"Yesterday," he said. "You?"

"Oh, I was born here. Can't wait to leave."

"How long have you worked at the café?"

"Since it opened, ten years ago."

"What about the steakhouse?" he asked. "How long has it been open?"

"The Woodbury? Five, maybe six years. I can't be sure."

"Isn't there another café in town?"

"You mean the Well Done?" she asked. "Yes, but it's only been there a couple of years. Nobody expects it to last."

"Why not?"

"The woman who owns it, Denise Parker," Laura said, "she's a stranger."

"And this town doesn't like strangers?"

"We like strangers like you," she said, "who come to town to spend money. But not like Denise, who come here and stay, thinkin' they'll be accepted."

"And why won't she be accepted?" Clint asked.

"I told you," she said. "She's a stranger." She stopped walking. "I live here."

Clint looked at the storefront, saw that it was a barber shop.

"You live here?"

"Upstairs," she said. "There's two rooms. I've lived here since I left my family's house."

"Well . . . what will you do with the rest of your evening?" he asked.

"Oh, take a bath, have something to eat . . . would you like to come up?"

"You don't even know my name," Clint said.

"Oh!" she said, as if it came as a surprise to her. "What is it?"

"Clint Adams."

Her eyebrows went up.

"I do know that name," she said. "You're famous."

"Some places."

"Only the whole West," she said. "And aren't there dime novels—"

"Yes, yes," he said. "I try to ignore those."

"If you come up," she said, "I'll make some . . . tea?"

"Tea?"

"I don't have anything stronger."

"Maybe another time, Laura," he said. "I still have some . . . things to do."

"Very well," she said. "I'll see you again, if you come back to the Lakewood to eat."

"I probably will," he said, "There are too many windows at the Woodbury."

"And don't bother with the Well Done," she advised.

"No?"

"No," she said. "You never know when something's gonna happen there."

"Like what?"

"Who knows?" she asked. "She's already had a bunch of her cooks beat up. Who knows what could be next?"

***

It seemed to Clint, if he wanted a good steak, he was going to have to go to the Woodbury, and take a chance on sitting in plain sight, where anyone could take a shot at him through the window.

If he knew for a fact that a steak at the Woodbury would be worth it, he might have risked it. But he didn't know that. So his only option seemed to be cooking the steak, himself.

That evening he walked to the Well Done, saw that a few tables were available, unlike the Woodbury and the Lakewood. Denise was still inside, scurrying around to both serve and cook.

"You're back," she said, when he walked in.

He was about to answer when he saw smoke coming from the kitchen.

"Something burning?" he asked.

She turned, saw the smoke, and then ran to the kitch-en.

Chapter Five

Clint followed her into the kitchen and saw the fire. It wasn't on the stove, but at the back door.

She turned. "Help," she yelled.

He went to the pump in her sink, worked it to fill a pot, then took it to the door and threw it on the flames. When he turned, she had filled a second pot and handed it to him while he handed her the first back. He tossed the water on the fire, turned and took the other pot from her again. The third time was the charm, and the fire was out.

"My God! That could've been a lot worse if not for you. Thank you."

"My pleasure," he said.

"I hope my customers didn't notice anything," she said.

"Why don't you go and find out," he said. "I'll look at the damage."

"Yes, all right. Thank you, again."

She went out into her dining room. Clint rushed to the back door, opened it, saw that it was still whole, although charred on the outside and in. There was also a broken window on the door, which someone had used to enter and start the fire.

He closed the door, found a mop and cleaned up the remnants of the water. He was finishing up when Denise came back into the kitchen.

"That mop suits you," she kidded.

"All dry," he said, setting it aside. "Someone broke in and started the fire. Luckily, it was a small one. Or it simply didn't have the time to spread."

"If you hadn't come . . ." she said, again. "Why *are* you here?"

"I wanted to borrow something."

"After what you did?" she said. "Anything."

"Your stove?"

"My . . . stove?"

"Yes," he said, "I want to make myself a steak."

"You don't want me to make it?"

"I thought I'd give you a break," he said. "You're doing the cooking and the serving so—"

"You didn't like the meal I cooked you last night," she said, cutting him off.

"Well . . . the steak could've been better."

"Sorry," she said, obviously stung, "it is rather hard to cook and serve, and I suppose I owe you . . . so yes, go ahead. Use my kitchen."

"I'll try to stay out of your way," he promised.

"That's all right," she said.

"Thank you."

"Here," she said, "let me get you started."

She grabbed a large, white apron, stood behind him and started tying it on.

"No, I don't need—okay, never mind. Thank you."

"You can hang your gun over there," she said, indicating a peg on the wall.

"I'll keep it on."

"In the kitchen?"

"I keep it on all the time," he said.

She stared at him.

"It suddenly occurs to me I never found out your name."

"It's—"

"No, no," she said, "don't tell me now. Just go ahead and cook your meal. I've got some customers."

There was room on the stove for four pans, so they each used two burners. At one point she reentered the kitchen after serving a table and saw him with a plate in his hand.

"I'll just take this out to a table and eat it—"

"Wait," she said. "Can I taste it?"

"Of course."

He put the plate down on a counter next to the stove. He had prepared a huge steak, smothered in onions, and surrounded by vegetables. She picked up a knife and fork, cut a piece, along with the onions, held it to her nose, and then put it into her mouth and chewed slowly.

"Oh God," she said, and her chewing increased. After she swallowed, she started to cut another piece.

"Whoa, whoa," he said, grabbing the plate, "my steak."

"That's the best steak I ever tasted," she said. "It's fragrant, tender, moist, the onions are heavenly—"

"Thank you," he said. "And now I'm going to eat it."

"Sure, go ahead. I've got two more tables and then I'll be done."

Clint left the kitchen and went to a back table with his plate, and a mug of coffee. He sat down and started eating. Denise was right. The steak was perfect.

Denise finished with her last two tables, then came over to him with a coffee pot.

"More?"

"Please."

She poured, then sat and poured herself some. She stared at his plate longingly.

"Okay," she said, "what's your name?"

"Clint Adams."

She stared at him.

"The Gunsmith cooks?" she said, in disbelief.

Chapter Six

Clint finished his meal while Denise sat across from him, drinking coffee.

"I have an idea," she said.

"What?"

"Come work for me," she said. "I can't pay much, but—"

"Work for you?" he asked. "As what?"

"A cook."

"Me? A cook in a restaurant?"

She pointed at his plate.

"That's the best steak I ever tasted," she said. "Can you cook anything else?"

"I've been a trail cook," he said. "Some biscuits, some beans and bacon—"

"Fish?" she asked.

"Well, yeah, I've cooked fish—"

"Venison?"

"On occasion, but—"

"Things are gettin' worse for me," she said. "They beat up my cooks and stole my supplies. Now they tried to set fire to my place. I need help Mr. Adams."

"Clint," he said.

"Clint. I can't fight them myself. I've been tryin', but I'm losin'. Maybe, with you as my cook, they'll stop trying."

He finished his meal and pushed his plate away.

"Peach pie?" she asked.

"Please."

She grabbed the plate, stood up to leave, then turned back.

"Did you like my peach pie yesterday?"

"Very much."

"You're telling me the truth, right?"

"I told you about your steak," he reminded her. "I think you're probably a better baker than you are a cook. Maybe that should be your specialty. Baked goods."

"Maybe you're right."

She went into the kitchen and came back with the pie and some more coffee.

"Would that take you out of competition with the Woodbury and the Lakewood?"

"Bakin'?"

He nodded.

"I don't think so," she said. "The Woodbury prides itself on its desserts."

"Still . . ."

"You think I can make a livin' with just baked goods?"

"After a while."

"Will you help me, Clint?"

He hesitated. So far only Laura, and Denise, knew who he was. And, of course, he had signed the hotel register under his real name.

"I tell you what," he said. "I'll work for you for a little while, until we know what's going on. And until you can get a baked good menu going."

"But?"

"We don't mention my name," he said. "If anybody asks, you have a new cook, but don't mention my name."

"Won't it get around town eventually that you're here?" she asked.

"Right now only three people know," he said. "I'm going to try to control that, but yes, eventually it will. Hopefully, somebody will try something before then, and I can catch them at it. Then we'll know who's been trying to drive you out."

"Yes!" she said. "And meanwhile, word will get out about your steaks."

"I hope you're right."

She reached out and dragged her finger through the remnants of his meal, then put the finger into her mouth.

"Don't worry," she said. "I am."

Chapter Seven

Clint and Denise agreed that he would start the next day. When he left, she locked the door, telling him she was going to clean up and then go home.

"Where's home?" he asked.

"There are a group of houses at the end of Spring Street," she said. "Mine is number five."

"Okay," he said. "As long as I know where to find you."

After he left, he walked back toward his hotel, but changed his mind and direction. He walked to the barbershop Laura lived above. There was a stairway on the side of the building. He went up and knocked. She looked surprised, but pleased, when she opened the door and saw him there. She was wearing a simple blue dress that made her blue eyes sparkle. Or maybe it was the smile doing that.

"Come in," she said.

"I just wanted to talk—"

"We can talk inside," she said.

She turned away from the door, so he had no choice but to follow her inside, closing the door behind him.

It was two rooms, as she had said. One was a small kitchen, and the other was a combination sitting and bedroom, with a small sofa, and a bed.

"Can I offer you anythin'?" she asked.

"No, I just ate."

"Oh, can I ask where?"

He hesitated, then said, "The Well Done Café."

"Why would you go there after I warned you not to?" she asked.

"I didn't think the other two places would let me into the kitchen."

"And she did?"

"Yes, and I cooked my own steak."

"Oh. How was it?"

"Delicious, but I'm not here to talk about what I ate."

"Really? Why are you here, then?"

"I introduced myself to you, you recognized my name."

"Of course I did," she said. "You're famous."

"Well," Clint said, "I'd like you to keep that to yourself for a while."

"Am I the only one who knows you're in town?"

"No, you're not," he said, "but I'm working on keeping the other people quiet, as well."

"Okay," she said, clasping her hands behind her back, "I suppose I could keep quiet . . ."

"Good."

". . . if you make me happy."

"What do I have to do to make you happy?" he asked.

"I think you know."

She unclasped her hands, unbuttoned the dress in front and slipped it off, leaving her standing there in just a camisole.

"Laura—"

"We haven't ever met before," she said, "but I know your reputation."

She slipped the straps off her shoulders and allowed the garment to fall to the floor. She was tall and slender, as he had known, but her breasts seemed solid, tipped with large, rosy nipples.

"Come on," she said, moving closer to him, "you've been on the trail for some time, right? You must be ready."

She came close enough for him to feel the heat from her naked body. Then she slid her hand down over his belt to his crotch.

"Oh yes," she said, rubbing him through his trousers, "you're ready . . ."

***

After Clint Adams left the Well Done Café, Denise locked the door and set about cleaning the place. When she was finished, she left by the front door, locking it behind her. She started for her house, but as she passed an alley between two stores, a man stepped out, grabbed her and dragged her inside. He clasped a hand over her mouth, muffling her screams.

In the alley he threw her to the ground, then knelt over her with a knife to her throat.

"Scream and I'll cut you from ear-to-ear."

"Wha-what do you want?" she asked.

"What everybody in town wants," he said. "For you to close your café and leave."

She knew that wasn't true. There were still some people who were eating in her café. But she knew she wouldn't get out of that alley alive if she didn't agree.

"A-all right," she said. "Tell whoever you're workin' for that I will."

The man laughed. She couldn't see his face in the dark alley, but she could smell his foul breath and body odor. And she felt his strength when he grabbed her.

"That's not good enough," he said. "I'm supposed to deliver a message."

"Wha-what kind of message?"

He reached for the front of her shirt and tore it open, also ripping the camisole underneath so that one breast bobbed free.

"This kind," he said.

***

Clint couldn't resist.

He took the naked girl into his arms and kissed her. Her mouth was hungry, her hands insistent. While the kiss went on, she grabbed at his clothes. Working together, they got him as naked as she was, with him setting his gun down close by the bed.

The kiss went on until she broke it so she could kiss his chest, and his belly and, finally, his hard, jutting cock. He allowed her to suck him for a short time, until he reached down, took her beneath her arms and lifted her to her feet for another kiss. Without breaking it, he lifted her into his arms and set her down on the bed.

"I can see one part of your reputation is well earned," she said, closing a hand around his hard penis. "But show me more!"

***

Her assailant reached out with his free hand and grasped her large breast, squeezing it tightly, painfully. She knew if she didn't do something, she was going to be raped.

As he bent his head to bite her nipple, she reached out, looking for something, anything to use as a weapon. Her hand closed over a piece of wood that felt solid enough. She grabbed it, then swung and hit him over the head.

"Ow, damn!" he swore, the knife coming away from her throat, and his other hand releasing her breast.

She managed to roll away from him, then clamber to her feet and run from the alley, holding her shirt closed over her bare breast as she ran. The few people on the street in that part of town turned to look, but no one made a move to help. When the assailant came staggering out of the alley, bleeding from the head, there were just enough people to convince him not to chase her. Instead, he went back into the alley to find his hat.

Chapter Eight

When she reached her house, Denise made sure all the doors were locked, then went to a small desk and took a gun from the top drawer. She peered out the window to see if she was followed, but there wasn't anyone. She tried to get her breathing under control. When she finally did, she went to the sink in the kitchen, set the gun right next to it, and washed off the dirt from the alley, as well as the man's hands. That done, she went to her bedroom, removed her torn garments and put on a clean shirt. After that she poured herself a brandy and sat on her sofa with the glass in one hand, and the gun in the other . . .

**

Clint and Laura rolled about on the bed together. More often than not, Clint found women, these days, more anxious to take control in bed. However, he was still old fashioned enough to believe the man should be in charge, so that resulted in a brief wrestling match. Eventually, though, he came out on top. He usually did.

He worked his way down her body with his mouth, enjoying the feel of her hot, smooth skin on his lips and tongue. When he got down between her legs, she was wet and waiting . . .

***

"Ow!" Dexter St. James snapped.

"Sit still," said the man bandaging his head. "This is what you get for letting a woman get the better of you."

"It wasn't my fault," Dex said. "You didn't tell me she had nice tits. When one of them fell out . . . well, I got distracted."

"So now you know Denise is an attractive woman," Doc Sentry said. "How does that change things?"

"It'll just make it more fun," Dex said.

Doc Sentry finished cleaning and bandaging the head wound and stepped back.

"You know you stink, right?" he asked.

Dex stood up and said, "I just got off the trail. I wanted to get the lay of the land before I had a bath and a meal."

"What'd you find out?"

"The lady can take care of herself," Dex said.

"So you might need help?"

"I doubt it. But if I do . . ."

". . . you'll get it. I can afford it."

"And do I have a good hotel room?" Dex asked.

"You do," Sentry said. "You're checked in to the Hotel Benedict."

"Thanks," Dex said. "I'll get a good night's sleep and start again in the mornin'."

"Very well."

Before leaving Dex asked, "What's the last thing you and your men pulled?"

"One of my men set fire to her back door today," Sentry said. "She managed to put it out pretty quick."

"See? She can take care of herself," Dex St. James said. "Yeah, this is gonna be real interestin'. I'll check in with ya when I get settled, Doc."

"You do that," Sentry said.

As St. James left the doctor's surgery a woman came in with a little boy, and Sentry asked, "Billy, what did you do this time?"

***

Laura screamed as waves of pleasure flowed over her body, and then Clint mounted her and drove his hard cock into her steamy depths.

She wrapped those long, lithe limbs around his waist and they moved together, the air in the room filling with the sound of their moist flesh slapping together.

After he exploded into her, he rolled off and they laid side-by-side, taking the time to catch their collective breath.

When she finally spoke, she said, "I told you to make me happy, but . . . Jesus!"

"Just trying to give the lady what she asked for," he replied.

"Well," she said, "I think I'm gonna have to return the favor."

"Give me a minute or two," he gasped, "and I'll take you up on that offer."

***

Denise finished her brandy, carried her gun and empty glass to the window again. Still nobody. She was fairly convinced now that the man from the alley wasn't coming for her again—not tonight.

But she kept the gun with her when she went to bed, wondering if she was going to have to ask Clint Adams to do more than cook for her?

Chapter Nine

Clint and Laura spent another hour getting to know each other's body, before he rose and began to dress.

"Slower," she said, from the bed. "I like to watch men get dressed."

Clint understood that. He truly enjoyed watching a lovely woman dress, slowly covering up everything he'd just spent hours enjoying.

The last thing he did was strap on his gun, then grab his hat.

"Remember what we talked about," he said.

"After what you just did to me?" she asked. "My brain is dead."

"Laura—"

"I remember, I know," she assured him, "I don't know who you are."

"Thank you."

"You will let me know when I remember who you are, right?" she asked.

"Absolutely." He kissed her. "Good-night."

"Good-night, stranger."

***

It was dark when he left, and that part of town was not well lit. Staying aware, he made his way back to the lighted part of town with the saloons still in full swing. But he wasn't in the mood to join the fray. He headed right back to his hotel, where the desk clerk he wanted was on duty.

"Can I help you, sir?" the young clerk asked.

"Yes," Clint said, "I'd like to know if you've told anyone that I checked in today?"

"Like who, sir?" the clerk asked, looking confused.

"Oh, your boss, the sheriff, a friend . . . anyone?"

"No, sir," he said, "I don't usually talk about the hotel's guests."

"That's good."

"But if you'll tell me your name again—"

"That's okay," Clint said, hoping the man was telling the truth and didn't know who he was.

"Is there anything I can do for you?"

"Not a thing," Clint said. "Everything's fine."

He went up to his room to turn in for the night.

***

The next morning, he was at the Well Done Café early—at least, he thought it was early, but when he got there the door was still locked.

He knocked on the door, peered in the window, but it seemed deserted. Remembering where Denise told him she lived, he headed that way.

She had said her house was number five, but he would have been able to pick it out, anyway. It was the only one that looked cared for. The others weren't falling down by any means, but they did look like a stiff wind might do them in.

Number five appeared to have gotten a new paint job and fence recently.

He went to the front door and knocked. Quickly, he saw a curtain in a front window move, and Denise peered out. Then the door unlocked and she opened it, with a gun in her hand.

"Come in! Quickly!" she snapped, looking harried.

He went in and she slammed the door, then locked it. When she turned to him, he pushed her hand with the gun away, so it wasn't pointing at him.

"What's going on?" he asked. "Why the gun?"

"A man attacked me last night while I was walkin' home," she said. "He dragged me into an alley, put a knife to my throat, and . . . and pawed me."

"Are you all right?"

"I hit him with a piece of wood and got away," she said. "And I've been carrying this gun around with me all night. Even slept with it."

"Did you get a good look at him?"

"No," she said, "but I smelled him. He smelled like he just got off a horse."

"Maybe he did," Clint said. "That's good, Denise. I can probably find him, if he rode in yesterday."

"Why find him?" she asked. "I wanna stay away from him."

"I want to know who sent him after you. I went to your café this morning, to start cooking."

"I—I was afraid to open up. Maybe . . . maybe I should close and leave town."

"On my first day as cook?" he complained. "I'm itching to get started."

"What about people findin' out who you are?"

"I think I've taken care of that, for now," he said. "Come on, get yourself ready and we'll walk over and open together."

"All right, Mr. Adams," she said.

"Clint," he said. "Just a cook named Clint."

"All right, Clint," she said. "I'll only be a minute."

Chapter Ten

When they got to the café there was nobody waiting outside for it to open.

"Not much of a breakfast rush," he said, as they entered.

"There never is," she said. "I usually get some business for supper, but that's about it."

"Well," he said, "when people taste my steak-and-eggs they'll be lining up to get in."

"I hope you're right."

"Let's get started and see."

They went into the kitchen, where Clint took off his hat, donned his apron, and began preparing to cook—only nobody came. He made a large pot of coffee anyway, to have it ready.

"Somebody will probably be along at lunch time," she said. "But certainly at supper."

"Then I don't get to make steak-and-eggs," he complained.

"But you will make those great steaks," she said. "And then word will get around."

At that point they heard somebody enter the café.

"Ah," she said, "maybe your first customer."

She started for the door, but stopped before stepping through.

"Let me have a look," he said.

He moved up beside her and peered out, saw a man and a woman at the door, looking around curiously.

"Looks like a husband and wife," he said. "You better get out there before they leave."

"Right."

She took a deep breath and went through the door. Clint watched as she seated the couple and took their order.

"You get to make one steak-and-eggs," she said, when she came back in.

"And?"

"Can you poach an egg?"

***

After a couple of hours, he had cooked two orders of steak-and-eggs, one poached egg, and one order of flapjacks.

There was an extra flapjack, which Denise decided to eat herself, because she hadn't had any breakfast. Clint had some eggs with her, and a hot biscuit.

"That was wonderful," she said. "You make those on the trail, over an open fire?"

"Oh yeah, all the time," Clint said.

"You must have a lot of people tryin' to sit around your fire."

"Actually," he said, "I usually eat alone."

"And do you get lonely?"

"On occasion. That's when I ride into town for some company."

"Women?" she asked.

"Sometimes a lady," he said, "sometimes a poker game. Sometimes just to see a friend."

"So why are you in Tenafly?"

"Drifting," he said. "I hadn't been to Montana in a while, and I like it in the Fall."

"So I'm keepin' you from movin' on," she said.

"That's okay," he said. "This is an interesting change for me."

As it got later several people came in, and Denise convinced them to go for the steak.

"You're a hit," she said later, when she brought in the dirty plates and put them by the sink. "Folks say they're gonna pass the word about your steaks."

"Good," he said, "maybe the word will get to the right people."

"Like the man who grabbed me last night?" she asked.

"Exactly," Clint said. "Let's see what happens if he comes after you, this time."

***

Dex St. James was actually right across the street from the Well Done at that moment, but Clint had no way of knowing that, since he was spending the entire time in the kitchen. The hired gun heard people coming out of the café talking about the steaks, and it got his curiosity up. But he didn't dare go in, not yet. It was too soon after he had tried to scare the woman the night before. So he simply kept watch for a while, to see how busy—or not busy—The Well Done Café really was. He was sure Doc Sentry was going to want to know.

***

"That's it," Denise said to Clint, at nine o'clock. "Time to clean up and go home. How did you like your first day as a cook?"

"I think the question is, how did *you* like my first day as a cook . . . boss?"

41

Chapter Eleven

Clint helped Denise clean the place before they left and closed up. He walked her back to her house and waited on the porch for her to unlock the door.

"Can you come in?" she asked.

"I was thinking of trying to find out who rode into town yesterday," he said, "and who it was that grabbed you."

"Could you come in first?" she asked. "I, uh . . ."

He realized she was afraid to go into her house.

"All right," he said, "let me go in and have a look around."

"Thank you," she said, filled with relief.

He went through the door first and walked through the house, turning up a couple of her lamps. Then he went back to the front door, where she was waiting just inside.

"It's all clear," he said.

"That's a relief," she said. "I keep thinkin' he's gonna come back."

"Let me see what I can find out," he said, "and then I'll come back later and check in on you."

"That would be great," she said.

"Meanwhile, you can keep your gun close."

"I will."

"And try not to shoot me when I come back."

"I'll do my best."

She followed him to the front door.

"Lock it as soon as I leave, and I'll knock three times when I come back."

"I'll be ready," she said. "I'm going to be bakin' some new recipes, so don't be surprised if I try them out on you when you get back."

"That gives me something to look forward to," Clint said. "I'll see you in a little while."

He went out the front door, waited there on the porch until he heard the lock turn, then headed toward the center of town.

***

There were two livery stables in town, and anybody who rode in the day before would have to put their horse up at one of them.

He found one stable still with the doors open, and the hostler told him that he hadn't had a stranger in there since Clint, himself.

While there he checked up on Eclipse, who seemed to have been fed and well-brushed. He stroked the big Darley's neck.

"Looks like we're going to be here longer than I thought, big fella," he said. "So you're going to get a lot of rest."

He went to the second stable, but found it locked up. He was going to have to try again in the morning.

He could've checked all the hotels and rooming houses in town for strangers, but that would've brought attention to himself. So he just went to his hotel room for the night.

***

The next morning, he went to Denise's house to walk her the to the café.

"I thought you were gonna come back last night," she said, when she opened the door.

"I thought I should turn in early so I could be here early," he said. "Did you get some sleep?"

"Yes," she said, "me and my gun. I suppose that's how you sleep, with your gun, every night?"

"It's always nearby," he said.

"Well, I had mine in my bed."

"That's not wise," he said. "You could roll over and shoot yourself. Just make sure it's within easy reach."

"Yes, okay."

"Should we walk to work, now . . . boss?"

***

Doc Sentry walked his patient out of his examining room to the front door and told her, "If the dizziness returns, come and see me right away."

"Thank you, Doc," the middle-aged woman said.

As she left, he turned and saw Dexter St. James sitting there.

"What've you got?" he asked.

"She's got herself a new cook," Dex said.

"Who is he?"

"I don't know."

"Any good?"

"I ain't had anythin' to eat there, but I watched a couple of people come out, talking about how good the steak was."

"Well, find out for me," Sentry said. "Go in and have a steak."

"I could do that."

"Will she recognize you?"

"No," he said, "it was dark in the alley."

"Wait," Sentry said. He reached up and removed the bandage from Dex's head. "Use your hat and your hair to cover that cut so she doesn't see it."

"Right."

"Let me know what happens."

Dex nodded and left the office. Doc Sentry put on his jacket and locked up behind him. He left a note on the door saying he'd be back in thirty minutes.

Chapter Twelve

There were a few more customers that morning, and then a few more in the afternoon.

"Word is gettin' around even faster than I thought," Denise said, coming into the kitchen later that day.

"Hey," Clint said, looking away from his stove, "weren't you going to make some cakes or something last night?"

"I made a few things," she said, "but you didn't come back."

"Maybe you should've brought them here today, tried them out on your customers."

"No, not until you taste them, first," she said. "You can do that tonight."

"All right."

"And weren't you gonna find out about the man who attacked me?"

"I checked both livery stables, and they had no strangers boarding their horses."

"So what's that mean?"

"It means he probably knew somebody in town who was able to board his horse for him."

"Did you talk to the sheriff?"

"No," Clint said, "I don't want the local law to know I'm here. Not just yet."

They heard somebody enter the café.

"Supper rush," she said, rolling her eyes.

Clint peered out of the kitchen, saw a man and woman with their two small children, and behind them, a large man, alone.

"Two tables," he said. "It is a rush."

"I'll take their orders," Denise said.

She went and seated the couple, and their children, then the other customer, the large man.

"Thank you," he said to her.

She thought the man looked vaguely familiar, but couldn't place him. If he was a stranger . . .

"Would you like to see a menu?" she asked.

"No, I heard you had a new cook who does a fine steak."

"That's right."

"Then that's what I'll have. And a beer."

"Comin' up, sir."

The family wasn't ready to order yet, so she went to the kitchen.

"Clint, I think it's him!" she hissed.

"Who?"

"The man who attacked me."

"That big man in there? You recognized him?"

"Well, no . . . I mean, yes . . . I mean, not exactly. But he's a stranger."

"What's he want?"

"A steak supper."

"Then let's give it to him," Clint said. "What about the family?"

"They're still lookin' over the menu."

"Well," Clint said, "take your time with them. He's not liable to try anything with that family here."

"But if he does, you'll kill him, right?"

"Take it easy," Clint said. "Let's make sure it's the right man before we talk about killing."

"Yes, all right," she said. "He wants a beer. Will you bring it to him?"

"Let's not make him suspicious, if it really is him," Clint said. "You take him a beer, and I'll watch from here."

"A-all right," she said.

She got a mug of beer and went back out to the dining room.

"There you go," she said, setting the beer down on his table. "Your steak is bein' cooked."

"Well, thank you, Ma'am," he said, politely.

"We're ready to order," the man with the family called from his table.

"Right away," Denise said. "Excuse me."

"Sure," the man said.

She went and took the family's order, then returned to the kitchen.

"Did you see him?" she asked.

"Yes, a big man," Clint said. "When his steak's ready, I'll take it to him."

"Good. Meanwhile, the family ordered . . ."

***

When the steak was cooked Clint smothered it with onions, added vegetables to the plate, then carried it to the table.

"Hey, you're the new cook?" the man asked.

"That's right."

"Well, I heard this steak was really good," the man said, picking up his knife and fork. "I'm lookin' forward to it."

"Enjoy," Clint said.

He went back to the kitchen, where Denise was standing at the stove, watching over the meals they were preparing for the family.

"What did you think?" she asked.

"He only seems to be after a steak," Clint said, "Let's see what he does when he's finished."

She frowned.

"He doesn't smell the same, but he's cleaned up," she said. "I just have a feeling it's him. Does he have a cut on his head?"

"Not that I noticed, but he's keeping his hat on," Clint said.

"Maybe we can get him to take it off," she said.

"Let me finish that," he said, replacing her at the stove. "You serve that family, and I'll keep an eye on the big man."

"I hope it's not him," she said, "but then again, I hope it is."

Chapter Thirteen

The family of four finished their supper, paid their bill and were leaving just as the big man was finishing his steak. Denise went back into the kitchen with the money, and Clint came out to talk to the stranger, the only diner left in the place.

"There ya are," he said, as Clint approached. "That was a great steak, my friend."

"Glad you liked it," Clint said. "Pass the word, if you get the chance."

"I will. Now, what about desert?"

"We have excellent apple and peach pie."

"Agh, peach," the man said, making a face. "I'll have the apple."

"Coming up."

Clint went into the kitchen and said to Denise, "It's got to be him."

"Why's that?"

"He doesn't like peach pie," Clint said. "Who doesn't like peach pie?"

"So . . . apple?"

"Yeah."

She cut a slice of apple pie and Clint took it and some more coffee to the table.

"Hey, friend," the man said, as Clint set them down, "can you have a seat and drink some coffee with me? I'd like to talk."

"Is that so?" Clint sat down, poured himself a cup of coffee. "What's your name . . . friend?"

"Dexter St. James," the man said. "Just rode into town yesterday. And now I've had the best damn steak I've ever had. I never expected to find that here."

"Don't you like surprises?"

"Once in a while they're fine," St. James said. "Actually, this one's okay." He had a bite of the apple pie. "You make this, too?"

"Nope," Clint said, "that was made by the lady who owns the café."

"Well, tell her good job," St. James said. "What's your name, friend?"

"Adam," Clint said.

"Adam what?"

"Adam the cook."

"Well, Adam the cook," St. James said, standing, "does this cover it?" He dropped some money on the table.

"That'll cover it, all right," Clint said. "Come back, again."

St. James took his hat off just long enough to run his fingers through his hair, then put it back on.

"Tell the lady I said thanks for the fine meal," he said, and left.

Clint picked up the money and went to the kitchen, where Denise was already cleaning up.

"It was him."

She turned and he handed her the money.

"How do you know?"

"He made the mistake of taking his hat off, just long enough for me to see the cut on his head."

"I knew it!" she said. "Do we know his name?"

"Dexter St. James."

"I never heard of him. Have you?"

"No," Clint said, "but if he's for hire, I can find out about him."

"And who hired him?"

"That might be a bit harder," Clint admitted, "but I can try."

"When?"

"Well," he said, "I do have a job . . . boss."

***

Dex St. James entered the doctor's office again, found the man sitting at a desk, writing something.

"What's on your mind, Dex?" Sentry asked.

"Steak."

"What about it?"

"The Well Done's new cook makes a great steak," St. James said.

"You ate there?"

"I did, just now."

"Did you meet the cook?"

"Yep."

Sentry waited, then said, "And?"

"His name's Adam."

"Adam what?"

"That's it," St. James said. "He said he was Adam the cook."

"Did she have other customers?" Sentry asked.

"Yes," St. James said, "and I heard some of them discussing the steak before I went in. I think word is gettin' around town."

Sentry put his pen down and stared at St. James.

"I don't want it getting around town," he said. "Do you understand?"

"Yeah, I understand," St. James said. "But . . ."

"But what?" Sentry asked.

"Would it be all right if I have one more of his steaks before I kill 'im?"

Chapter Fourteen

"What will you do?" Denise asked, as they walked to her house.

"Tomorrow morning, before I come to work," he said, "I'll send telegrams to some people I know. One of them is bound to have heard of this Dexter St. James, if he has any kind of reputation."

"And then what?"

"And then we'll know who and what we're dealing with."

"But not who hired him?"

"No," he said, "I'll still have to find that out."

When they reached her house, he took her key, unlocked the door and went in first. She stood just inside the door and waited.

"All clear," he told her, handing back the key.

"Stay," she said. "I have some pastries I made. We'll eat them with coffee, and you tell me what you think."

"You know," he said, "I'm not really a cook."

"You could've fooled me," she said. "Everybody loved your food. They're all tellin' me to give their compliments to the new cook."

"Really?"

"I just need your opinion of my bakin'," she said. "Before I bring it into the café."

"Okay," Clint said. "I'll stay. You bake, and I'll stay, for a while."

She smiled.

"That's great," she said. "That means I can move around my kitchen without carryin' a gun."

"That's right," he said. "I'll carry the gun."

***

Denise set Clint up in her living room with a cup of coffee and then, one by one, brought out cakes, pies and pastries for him to try.

Finally, she came out of the kitchen and sat down beside him with a cup of tea she made for herself.

"What did you think?"

"I think I put on ten pounds," he said, "but it was all great."

"Really?"

"Those little cakes," he said. "What are you going to call them?"

"They're called *petit fours*."

"What?"

"It's French," she said. "I learned about them back East."

"So you're going to bring French cakes to the West?"

"I guess so," she said. "It would make me very differ-ent from the other two restaurants."

"Yes, it would."

"Maybe I could even become a bakery, and just do baked goods. Then, maybe, nobody would be tryin' to shut me down."

"We'd have to find out why they're trying to shut you down," he said. "Because of who you are, or what you do."

"I see," she said.

Clint leaned forward and took another *petit four*, popped it into his mouth.

"Eleven pounds," he said, and they laughed.

***

Dexter St. James wasn't staying in the hotel anymore, or a boarding house. He was staying in Doc Sentry's house, which was outside of town. His horse was in a small barn next to the house.

He was in the house while the doctor was out deliver-ing a baby. Left alone, he started to figure out how he would kill Adam the cook, and how he'd make it look.

"I don't care how you get rid of him," Sentry had said, "just get it done."

St. James hated the thought of killing somebody who could cook a steak the way he did, but he didn't have much choice, since he was being paid.

St. James prowled the doctor's house, found a room with bookshelves lining the walls, a leather chair, a desk, and a sideboard with some decanters on it. He checked them and finally poured himself a glass of brandy. He took it to the leather chair and sat. The doctor had told him to make himself "at home."

"Sir?"

He looked at the doorway, saw the doctor's housekeeper standing there. She was a young black woman in her twenties who appeared a little heavy in the hips and bust, which was something St. James didn't mind in a woman. She wore a gingham cotton dress that clung to her healthy body.

"Can I get you somethin'?" she asked. "The doctor, he tol' me to make sure you was comfortable."

"What's your name?" St. James asked.

"Opal."

"Well, Opal," he said. "I do have a way you can help me get more comfortable—if you're up for it."

"Anyt'ing, sir," she said. "I am to make you comfortable, or lose my job."

"Well, then," he said, "let's start with that dress . . ."

Chapter Fifteen

"I better get going," Clint said. "I have things to do in the morning."

"Do you have to go?" she asked.

She had cleared the room of cakes and coffee, and they were sitting there talking about new dishes for the café.

"We should both get some sleep, Denise."

"Do you have a girl waitin' for you at your hotel, Clint?" she asked.

"A girl? No," he said. "Just an empty hotel room."

"Then why not stay here?" she asked. "For the night."

"Are you still scared?" he asked. "I guess I could sleep on the sofa—"

"That would be great!" she said, cutting him off before he could say more. "I'd sleep much easier with you in the house."

"Okay," he said, "but then I'll have to leave early to go to my hotel and get dressed for work."

"I'll make sure you get up," she said. "I'll even make you an early breakfast."

"Well," he said, "all right, then. Sounds like a plan."

***

When Doc Sentry came home that night, he immediately heard the sounds coming from his library office. He walked down the hall and peered in. Dexter St. James had a naked black woman down on all fours and was plunging into her from behind. Sentry saw the wide hips, large buttocks and pendulous breasts and recognized his housekeeper, Opal. She was grunting each time St. James slammed his cock into her. When the gunman looked up and saw Sentry, he smiled and raised his eyebrows.

Doc Sentry withdrew, went back up the hall to his sitting room, where he poured himself a brandy. He couldn't very well fire the girl, he had told her to make St. James comfortable any way she could. And he couldn't fire St. James, because he had told the man to make himself at home.

He sat in an armchair with his drink and waited for them to finish.

***

Denise made up the sofa for him with a blanket and some pillows. He told her not to bother with a sheet, he'd be all right on the cushions. She said good night and went to her bedroom.

Clint took off his shirt, boots and socks, but decided to sleep with his trousers on, just in case. He also set the gunbelt close by, within easy reach, then settled down on the sofa. When his head hit the pillow, he fell asleep—but not so soundly that the slightest noise wouldn't wake him.

He sat up and reached for his gun in the darkness.

"It's just me," Denise said. "Don't shoot."

"What are you doing sneaking around?" he asked.

"I couldn't sleep, and I didn't want to wake you. I thought a glass of brandy might—"

"Let's light the lamp," he said, rising from the sofa. He walked to the gas lamp, struck a match and lit the wick. When he turned it up, she was bathed in the light, standing there . . . naked.

"Oh," he said.

"I thought you'd be sound asleep," she said.

The lamp caused shadows, which highlighted the opulent curves of her body.

"Brandy?" she asked.

"I can think of another way to get you tired enough to sleep," he said.

She smiled.

"I was hopin' you'd say that."

***

The first one to come down the hall was Opal. She looked embarrassed, but stopped and asked, "Would you like some'ting to eat, doctor?"

"Just a snack, Opal," he said. "Maybe a sandwich and some coffee."

"Yes, sir."

"And Opal?"

"Yes, sir?"

"Next time you want to entertain my guest," he said, "don't do it in my library, all right?"

"Yes, sir," she said. "Sorry, sir." She rushed away to the kitchen.

Moments later Dexter St. James appeared, his shirt on but unbuttoned, carrying his gunbelt in his hand.

"Sorry about that, Doc," he said. "Don't blame the girl."

"I don't," Sentry said.

"Can I have one of those?" St. James asked.

"Pour it yourself."

"Thanks."

St. James went over, poured himself a glass, then came back and sat on the sofa.

"My people want this taken care of quickly," Sentry said. "Can you do that?"

"Sure," St. James said, sipping his drink. "Just as soon as I have another steak."

Chapter Sixteen

Denise turned and walked back to her bedroom. Clint grabbed his holster, slid the gun into it, then followed her. She had turned up the lamp next to the bed, just a bit. As he entered, she turned to face him. She had a lovely body, smooth skin, bountiful curves, pale nipples.

"Here," she said, "let me do that."

She took his holster and hung it on the bed post.

"Is that all right?"

"That's fine."

She moved close to him, put her hands on his hips.

"Now let's get rid of these," she said, and began to undo his trousers.

He waited until he was fully naked before putting his hands on her, running his palms over her silky skin. When his hands brushed her nipples, she caught her breath and closed her eyes. She reached down and grasped his hard penis with one hand, began stroking it gently.

He pulled her closer, then, and kissed her. She'd cleaned up before getting ready for bed, but had not had a bath. Neither had he, so they both still had kitchen smells on them—spices, fried meats.

"I almost did this in the kitchen, at the restaurant," she said, into his ear as their hands roamed, "but I was afraid we might get caught."

"Much better here," he said, sliding his hands down to cup her firm buttocks.

They kissed again, then lowered themselves onto her bed.

***

Dexter St. James watched as the door to his bedroom opened and Opal eased in. He was reclining on the bed, clad only in his underwear, smoking a cigarette, waiting.

"Where's the Doc?" he asked.

"Asleep," she said.

She walked to the foot of his bed, and dropped her dress to the floor, revealing herself to be naked underneath. She had big breasts, wide hips, dark chocolate nipples, and a dark, curly patch between her heavy thighs.

"Did you get into trouble?" he asked.

"No," she said, getting onto the bed at the bottom and crawling up to him on all fours. "He just tell me not to use his liberry again."

"You have a funny accent," St. James said. "Where are you from?"

"Jamaica."

"Where's that? The West?"

"It is another country," she told him, running her hand along his bare thigh.

"Wait," he said, lifting his hips and removing his underwear so that his big cock flopped into view. "There you go."

She let her hand move up his thigh, stroked his belly, then his penis, which began to stir.

"It was hard," he told her, "but I've been waitin' for you for so long it got soft."

"I had to clean the kitchen, and then wait for him to go to bed," she said, running her forefinger along the length of him. "But don't worry, mon. I can get it hard again."

She leaned over and, this time, licked the length of his cock.

"Oh yeah," he said, "you can . . ."

***

Denise was flat on her back, her legs spread wide to accommodate Clint, who had settled down on his stomach between them, his face pressed to her fragrant crotch.

"Oh God," she groaned, as he used his tongue to trace her moist vagina.

When she was so wet she was gushing, he changed position, climbed atop her and drove himself deeply into her. Her eyes went wide and her mouth opened, but no sound came out. When he started to press in and out of her, she moved her butt in unison. Rather than wrap her legs around his waist, as many women had done in the past, she left them splayed out, and dug her heels into the mattress. Her arms were spread wide, and her hands closed into fists with wads of the sheet clasped in her fingers. She grunted as they slammed their bodies together . . .

***

"Do you not like my face, Mr. Dex?" Opal asked, while St. James drove into her wet pussy from behind.

"I like your face just fine," he said, in between grunted. "I . . . just . . . like . . . your . . . big . . . ass . . . better!"

He continued to drive in and out until he felt his explosion coming, then rammed his cock all the way into her and ejaculated . . .

Chapter Seventeen

Clint woke the next morning to the smell of bacon. He was not happy that Denise had managed to leave the bed and go to the kitchen without alerting him. He had to remind himself of who he was, Clint Adams, not Adam the cook. One moment of letting down his guard could result in death.

Stupid, stupid . . .

He rose, washed, dressed and strapped on his gun. Only then did he go to the kitchen.

"Well," Denise said, "you look like you're ready for work."

She was still wearing a nightgown.

"I'm ready for that hearty breakfast you promised me," he said, sitting at the kitchen table.

"Comin' up," she said. "Meanwhile, start on this." She put a mug of coffee in front of him.

"Thanks."

She went to the stove, picked up a spatula and, after a few flips, turned back with a plate laden with eggs, bacon, and flapjacks.

"Is that hearty enough for you?" she asked.

"It would be if there were some biscuits," he kidded.

She turned, then came right back with a basket of biscuits.

"Anythin' else?" she asked.

"Yes," he said, "sit and eat with me."

"My pleasure."

She made up a plate for herself and sat across from him.

"Sorry," she said, "no steak."

"That's okay," he said. "I'm the steak guy, remember?"

"How could I forget," she said. "Two days and the word has already spread. I think we're going to be busy today."

"Then I better get my telegrams sent and get to work," he said. "I can walk you there—"

"I think I'll be okay in broad daylight," she said. "Especially since I'll be able to recognize that man—St. James?"

"Yes, Dexter St. James. Hopefully, by tonight, I'll have some information on him."

"Then you send your telegrams and I'll see you at the café."

"It won't take long," Clint said. "I should be there for the breakfast rush."

"I'm looking forward to it."

***

Clint found the telegraph office and sent two telegrams, one to Rick Hartman in Labyrinth, Texas, the other to Talbot Roper in Denver, Colorado.

Hartman owned a saloon in Labyrinth, the town Clint called home if there was any. He stopped there often to rest and relax, and usually spent a lot of time with Hartman, who had connections all over the country by keeping his eyes and ears open. If anyone knew anything about Dexter St. James it would be Rick.

Talbot Roper, who was probably the best private detective in the country, worked out of Denver, and whatever Rick didn't know, Talbot would.

One or both of his friends would get back to him with something.

***

When St. James came down for breakfast Doc Sentry was already at the table. Opal came out of the kitchen with platters of food, smiled at St. James as she set them down.

"Coffee?" she asked him.

"You bet."

He sat down and began to fill his plate with eggs and meats, potatoes and flapjacks and biscuits.

"Good-morning, St. James," Sentry said.

"Doc."

"Did you have a good night?"

"Slept like the dead," St. James said, then added, "when I slept."

Opal came in, set his coffee down in front of him, smiled again and left.

"If you ruin my housekeeper—" Sentry started.

"Housekeeper and cook?" St. James asked. "This food is great. Doesn't seem like I did her any harm."

"Keep it that way," Sentry said. "My partners are anxious for you to do your job."

"Do I ever get to see who your partners are?" St. James asked.

"That's not necessary," Doc Sentry said. "Let's just say I'm the managing partner. I'm the one who tasks you and pays you."

"And pays me well," St. James reminded him.

"Once the job is done," Sentry reminded him.

"Yeah, right," St. James said, with his mouth full, "right after we plow through all this food."

Chapter Eighteen

When Clint got to the Well Done more than half the tables were occupied.

"Thank God," Denise said, when she entered the kitchen. "They all want your steak-and-eggs."

"Then let's give it to them," he said, putting on his apron.

He did his best to catch up to the orders, getting four pans going at the same time, and Denise rushed them out to the diners. Before long she came into the kitchen looking relieved.

"Everybody got fed, and loved it," she said.

Clint had one pan still going, emptied the contents onto a plate and handed it to Denise.

"The last one. I guess now we can get ourselves ready for the lunch rush."

"I imagine there are some people in town who aren't happy about this," she said, "but the ones eatin' here are very happy . . ."

She rushed out to deliver the last breakfast, then came hurrying back in.

". . . thanks to you," she finished.

***

"The Gunsmith?" Larry Nelson's brother asked.

"I swear, Danny," Larry said. "It was him, big as day, and wearin' an apron."

"How do you know?" Danny Nelson asked.

"I've seen him before, in Wichita, once," Larry said. "It's him."

"And he's cookin' in a café?"

"And cookin' real good, too," Larry said. "Best breakfast I ever had."

Both men were at their jobs, working in a carpenter's shop.

"You tell anybody else?" Danny asked.

"Not a soul," Larry said to his older brother. "I wanted to tell you first."

"Well, keep it to yourself, Larry," Danny said.

"What are you gonna do?" Larry asked.

"I'll have a talk with Sheriff Lariman," Danny said. "See what he has to say about it."

"What can he say?" Larry asked. "Won't he be happy that Clint Adams is feedin' people, and not shootin' 'em?"

"We'll see."

***

"Are you spreadin' this around?" Lariman asked Danny Nelson, later in the afternoon.

"No, I ain't," Danny said, "and I tol' my brother to keep quiet about it, too."

"Okay, keep it that way."

"How come you didn't look surprised?" Danny asked.

The lawman ran the arthritic fingers of his left hand through his hair.

"Frank, from the telegraph office, came over and told me," he said. "Adams sent a couple of telegrams, this mornin'."

"To who?"

"That ain't none of your business, Danny," Lariman said. "Just keep quiet about this, you hear. If word gets around, I'll know it was you or your brother,"

"What about Frank?"

"I told him the same thing," Lariman said. "First one who talks gets thrown in jail."

"What fer?" Danny asked.

"Disturbin' the peace," Lariman said. "Mine!"

***

"Clint Adams?" Doc Sentry asked. "Are you sure, Sheriff?"

"No, I'm not sure," Lariman said. "I've only heard it. I'm gonna go over there and check it out. But I thought you'd like to know, Doc."

"Thanks, Jack," Sentry said. "Let me know as soon as you confirm it."

"I will."

Lariman put his hat on and left the house. As soon as the door closed, Dexter St. James came out of hiding.

"You heard?" Sentry asked.

"I heard."

"What do you think?"

St. James rubbed his jaw.

"The cook was wearin' a gun when he came out of the kitchen," St. James said. "I thought it was odd, at the time." He snapped his fingers. "And his name!"

"Adam the cook," Sentry said.

"That would explain why he didn't wanna give a full name," St. James said.

"So the Gunsmith has changed careers?" Sentry asked. "He's now a cook?"

"That could be."

"No," Sentry said, "I think it's more likely Miss Parker has hired herself a gun."

"Clint Adams is a gun, that's for sure, Doc," St. James said, "but I never heard of him hirin' out."

"Like we said," Sentry said. "Maybe he's changed."

"I'll find out," St. James said.

"No," Sentry said. "Don't do anything until we hear from the sheriff. I want it confirmed that we're dealing with The Gunsmith."

Chapter Nineteen

Sheriff Lariman walked into the Well Done Café and saw that they had something unusual going on—a lunch rush.

"Sheriff," Denise said, as he stopped just inside the door. "What brings you here?"

"I've been hearin' things about a new cook," Lariman said. "I thought I'd come and see for myself."

"Of course," she said. "Let me show you to a table."

He followed her across the room and sat.

"A menu?" she asked.

"I've been hearin' somethin' about a steak?" he said.

"Yes," she said, "a wonderful steak. It's our new cook's specialty. Is that what you'll have?"

"I might as well try the man's specialty, right?" he asked.

"You won't be disappointed," she said. "Coffee or beer?"

"Coffee," he said. "I'm still on duty." He took off his hat. Denise noticed that the man's hands were twisted with arthritis.

"Sheriff, would you like the steak to be . . . sliced for you?"

Lariman smiled sadly and held out his hands so they could both look at them.

"Age is a terrible thing, Miss Parker," he said, "but I think I can still manage a knife and fork. But thank you for askin'."

"I'll bring your order out quickly, Sheriff," she promised.

She hurried into the kitchen and grabbed Clint's arm.

"What is it?" he asked.

"The Sheriff's out there," she said. "He wants a steak."

"That's not a problem," Clint said.

"He's never eaten here before," she said. "Why now?"

"You said the word was getting around," Clint said. "Why does he say he's here?"

"He says he heard about your steak."

"Well, there you are," he said. "We'll just give him a good one so he can taste for himself."

"Okay," she said.

"Relax, Denise," he said. "Bring the man what he wants to drink. And then come back in and tell me about him."

"Yes, all right," she said. "He wants coffee."

"A man after my own heart," he said.

"Maybe not," she said, and left the kitchen with the lawman's coffee.

***

Sheriff Lariman couldn't believe how good the meal was. Especially if the cook really was the Gunsmith. But that was what he had actually come to the Well Done to find out.

When Denise came back to the table to get his empty plate, she asked Lariman, "Dessert, Sheriff?"

"Is that also made by your new cook?" he asked.

"Sorry," she said, "the bakin' is all done by me."

"Well, I tell you what," he said, "you have your new cook bring me out a piece of his favorite pie. Plus, I'd like to meet 'im."

"I'll tell 'im," she said.

"And some more coffee."

"Comin' up."

She went to the kitchen and said to Clint, "He wants you to bring him a piece of pie so he can meet you."

"Cut it," Clint said, "and I'll take it."

Denise sliced a piece of peach pie, put it on a plate, and handed it to Clint with a pot of coffee. Clint carried both out to the sheriff's table. The other diners had left, either because they were done, or because of the sheriff.

"Here you go, sheriff," Clint said.

"Lariman, Mr. Adams," the lawman said. "My name is Sheriff Lariman. Have a seat . . . please."

Clint sat across from the man.

"What brings the Gunsmith to Tenafly, Mr. Adams?" Lariman asked.

"Cooking," Clint said. "I heard Denise opened a new place and needed a cook. Seems her employees keep getting beat up. You know anything about that, Sheriff?"

"Sure," Lariman said, "I looked into it each time it happened."

"And?"

"The cooks said they didn't know who did it, and then promptly left town."

"I see."

"You know," Lariman said, "the word's gotten around town about her new cook."

"And now you're going to spread the word that it's me?" Clint asked.

"Hell, no," Lariman said. "If folks come here, I want it to be for the steak, not to try you out. Besides, I might wanna come back here for a steak." He put a piece of pie into his mouth. "And this pie ain't bad, either."

Chapter Twenty

"What'd he say?" Denise asked Clint when he came back into the kitchen.

"He enjoyed the steak."

"And?"

"And he's not going to give me away."

"No," she said, "I meant, what about the pie?" She grinned.

"He liked that, too."

She pulled a chair over and sat down.

"We've got some time before supper."

"Are you suggesting what I think you're suggesting?" he asked.

"No!" she said. "I just want to talk."

"Go ahead," he said, leaning back against the stove, then straightening quickly because it was still hot.

"Do you believe him?" she asked.

"You haven't done what I asked you to do, yet."

"What's that?"

"Tell me about him?"

"He's been a lawman for a long time," she said, "but his best days are behind him. You see his hands?"

"I did," Clint said. "Pretty bad arthritis. He probably won't be able to hold onto his badge much longer."

"Which means he might be lookin' for some retirement money," she said.

"So you think he's in somebody's pocket."

She nodded.

"That's why he never found out who's tryin' to put me out of business when my cooks kept gettin' beat up."

"And that's why you didn't bother going to him about the fire."

"Yes," she said, "but you'll notice he never came around to ask about it, either."

"Town lawmen are usually under the thumb of either the mayor, or some wealthy rancher."

"Neither, in this case," she said. "The mayor's a good man, and we really don't have wealthy ranchers livin' near here."

"That's good to know," Clint said. "So then we should look at the people in town who would benefit from your place closing down. That would be the owners of the Woodbury Steakhouse or the Lakewood Café."

"And I don't know either one of them," she admitted.

"I guess I'll have to find out who they are and introduce myself."

"As the new cook here?"

"To start with . . ." he said.

***

To Denise's pleasure they had a supper rush, and right in the middle of it one of the diners, a man on his own, said to her, "Can I talk to the cook? This steak is excellent."

"He's a little busy at the moment," she said.

"That's all right," he said. "I'll have dessert and wait. I'd really like to meet him."

"Who should I tell him is interested?" she asked.

"My name's Custis Delaney," the man said. "I own the Woodbury Steakhouse."

"Mr. Delaney," she said, "I own this place. My name is Denise Parker."

"Well, Miss Parker, excuse me for mistaking you for a waitress. I'm very happy to meet you." He stood up and shook her hand. He was tall, broad-shouldered, with a hint of grey at the temples of his black hair. "I hope you don't mind if I talk to your cook. In fact, I'm going to try and steal him."

"You can try," she said.

"You're pretty confident I'll fail, then?" he asked.

"Yes, I am."

"Well, good," he said. "I'll have a piece of your pie, and some coffee."

"What kind of pie?"

He smiled.

"You choose."

"Comin' up."

Denise hurried to the kitchen, feeling more trepidation than she was showing.

Clint saw the look on her face as he glanced up from his stove.

"What is it?"

"Remember you said you were gonna find out who owns the Woodbury?"

"Yes, and the Lakewood."

"Well, the Woodbury is here, lookin' for you. His name is Custis Delaney."

"Custis?"

"That's what he said."

Clint had only ever known one other man named Custis, and that was a Deputy Marshal known as Longarm, Custis Long.

"What's he want?" Clint asked.

"He enjoyed his steak," Denise answered, "and he came right out and told me he was gonna try to steal you away from me."

"Well, let him try."

She smiled. "That's what I told him. He's gonna have pie and wait to see you at the end of the night."

"Let him wait, then," Clint said. "We've still got people to feed."

Chapter Twenty-One

"That's it," Denise said, later. "Delaney's the only one left in the dining room."

"Then let's both go and talk to him," Clint said.

"He wants to talk to you," she said.

"Well, I work for you," he answered, "so he'll talk to both of us."

They left the kitchen together and walked to Delaney's table, where the man was till drinking coffee.

"Mr. Delaney," she said, "this is Adam, my cook."

"Adam?" The man stood and extended his hand. "Adam . . . who?"

"Just Adam," Clint said, shaking the man's hand.

Delaney was obviously curious about the gun on Clint's hip.

"Can we sit and talk, Adam?" he asked.

"As long as Denise sits with us," Clint said.

"Of course."

Delaney reached out and pulled another chair over so Denise could sit.

"The steak I had tonight was amazing," he said, "and I run a steakhouse."

"I appreciate that," Clint said.

"I have several cooks working for me, and I'd like to add you to my team," Delaney said. "I'm sorry, Miss Parker, but I think I can pay him more."

"Hey, it's up to him," Denise said.

"As for you," he went on, "that pie was wonderful. So why don't you close this place down, and both come and work for me?"

That came as a surprise. Clint looked at Denise, and wondered if she was tempted to simply work for Custis Delaney and bake?

"I don't know about Adam," she replied, immediately, "But my answer is no. I like ownin' my own place."

"You've had some trouble here, I heard," Delaney said. "Can't keep your cooks, your suppliers, even had a fire?"

"I'll survive all that, Mr. Delaney," she said. "If any of that was your doin'—"

"Whoa, whoa," Delaney said, putting his hands up, "that's not how I do business. Sure, I'll try to steal a cook, but I don't have them beat up and driven out of town, and I do not start fires."

He stood up, as if he was so insulted he had to leave.

"Adam, you don't have to give me an answer now," he said. "Think it over."

"I have," Clint said. "The answer is no."

Delaney looked at each of them in turn.

"You're both making a big mistake," he said. "But Miss Parker, I wish you luck."

"I don't need luck," she said. "I have Adam."

"And her baking," Clint said. "That's going to become real popular."

"I'm curious," Delaney said, to Clint, "why the gun?"

"I just want to make sure the cow is dead before I cook it," Clint said.

***

After Delaney left, Denise locked the door, and they cleaned up together.

"Were you tempted?" Clint asked.

"By what?" Denise asked.

"Delaney's offer," he said. "To bake for him at the Woodbury?"

"No," she said. "Were you?"

"I'm not really a cook, so no," Clint said.

"Do you think he's responsible for the things that've been happenin'?"

"He seemed to actually be insulted when you mentioned the fire," Clint said. "The other things, maybe, but I don't think he had anything to do with the fire."

"So then that might leave the owner of the Lakewood," she suggested.

"Yes," Clint said, "I'm going to find out who that is."

"How?"

"The simple way," he said. "By asking."

"At the Lakewood?"

"No," he said, "the next best thing. I'll ask a bartender."

***

"It's him," Sheriff Lairman told Doc Sentry.

"You're sure?"

"Oh yeah," Lariman said. "He didn't bother to deny it."

"What the hell is the Gunsmith doing in Tenafly?" Sentry asked. "And why is he cooking at the Well Done?"

"He's lookin' for a change?" Lariman asked.

"No," Sentry said, "she hired him."

"He was wearin' his gun in the kitchen, while he cooked," Lariman said.

"Yeah," Sentry said, "she hired herself a gun."

"Well," Lariman said, "so did you."

Chapter Twenty-Two

After Lariman left Doc Sentry's house, Dexter St. James came down and joined the Doc in his library.

"So now what?" he asked.

Sentry, sitting in his armchair, looked up at his hired gun.

"Can you take the Gunsmith?" he asked.

"Of course."

"Alone?" Sentry asked. "The man's a legend."

"With creaky bones," St. James said. "Don't worry, I can handle him."

"I don't want him killed as The Gunsmith."

"What?"

"That would attract too much attention," Sentry said. "I want Adam the cook killed."

"Do you know what it would mean to my reputation for me to kill the Gunsmith?" St. James asked.

"Do you want an increase in your reputation," Doc asked, "or an increase in my money?"

"I guess that would depend on how much money we're talkin' about," St, James said.

"Sit down and have a drink," Sentry said, "and we'll talk about it."

***

Clint walked Denise home, stopped at the front door, took the key and checked out the house.

"Clear," he said.

"Are you coming in?" she asked, placing her hand on his chest.

"Not right now," he said. "I've got to ask some questions."

"About who owns the Lakewood?"

"Yes. And I have to check at my hotel for replies to my telegrams."

"Come by later, then," she said. "We'll have coffee and cakes."

"I'll be there," he said.

She kissed his cheek and he left the house.

He walked to his hotel and stopped at the front desk.

"Any messages for me?" he asked the clerk.

"Yes, sir," the clerk sad. "Two telegrams." The young man handed them over.

"Thank you."

"Sir?"

"Yes?"

"About your name . . ."

"I'd still like you to keep it to yourself."

"I just wanted to tell you, the sheriff was here, looking at the register."

"Thanks for telling me that," Clint said, and handed the young man a dollar.

"Thank you!"

He took the telegrams to his room and read them there. Both Rick Hartman and Talbot Roper had things to say about Dexter St. James. He read both telegrams twice, then folded them and tucked them away.

Clint decided toiling in a kitchen all day meant he needed a bath in the evening. After the desk clerk arranged it, he took a quick one and then headed over to the Whiskey River Saloon. By the time he got there, it was getting dark, and the usual saloon activities—drinking and gambling—were in full swing.

"Get that good meal?" the bartender asked. "Haven't seen you back here since then."

"Yeah, I did, thanks," Clint said. "How about a beer?"

"Comin' up."

When the bartender set the beer down in front of him, Clint said, "Maybe you can help me with something."

"I'll try."

"The Lakewood Café," Clint said. "Do you know who owns it?"

"Sure do."

"Can you tell me his name?"

"I can tell you his name and point 'im out," he said. "Jim Longworth, and he's right over there."

Clint turned and looked at the gaming tables.

"Faro or poker?" he asked.

"Poker. Guy with the suit. Owns a restaurant, but dresses like a gambler."

"Thanks."

Clint picked up his beer and carried it across the room to the poker table. There were no empty chairs, so he watched for a while. Sometimes you could learn a lot about a man by watching him play poker.

Clint watched eight hands. Longworth won five of them. On the hands he lost, he bluffed, then laughed about it. The other four players at the table didn't like him.

"Jim Longworth?" Clint finally said.

"You been watchin' the game for a while. Finally decided to speak up?"

"Can we talk?"

"That depends on who you are," Longworth said, not looking up from his cards.

"I'm the new cook over at the Well Done Café."

Longworth looked at him then, said, "Deal me out," tossed his cards and stood.

"Let's talk," Clint said.

Chapter Twenty-Three

They went to the bar and Clint asked the bartender for two more beers.

"Thanks," Longworth said, picking his up. "I've been hearin' somethin' about you and steak."

"I cook them," Clint said.

"I'll have to come over and try one."

"Sure thing," Clint said. "We'll take care of you. In fact, we had Mr. Delaney over there today."

"That guy!" Longworth said. "You gotta watch out for him."

"Well, he liked my steak so much he offered me a job."

"That figures," Longworth said. "He's always tryin' to steal my cooks."

"And what about you?" Clint asked. "Ever try to steal a cook? Or drive one out of town?"

"Never, on either count," Longworth said. "My cooks are just fine. But I heard your boss was having some trouble. I feel bad for her, but you have to deal with things like that when you have your own business."

"I guess so."

"Oh, believe me," Longworth said. "I know so. When I opened, Delaney tried to drive me out."

"How?"

"Scare my cooks, steal my supplies."

"Start any fires?"

"What? No. We've never had any fires."

"Lucky. We had one, purposely set."

"That's bad," Longworth said. "Hope there wasn't much damage."

"We managed to put it out," Clint said.

"So what's your name?" Longworth asked.

"Adam," Clint said, "the cook. Thanks for talking to me."

"Sure. I've got to get back to the game."

"Maybe you shouldn't bluff so much," Clint suggested.

"I know, that's a flaw in my game. You play?"

"Some."

"Come by and play, some time."

"I will," Clint said. "Thanks."

He put his half-finished beer down on the bar and left.

***

I never heard of Jim Longworth," Denise said.

They were seated in her kitchen, with coffee and cakes in front of them.

"Well, he says when he opened The Lakewood, Delaney tried to drive him out."

"So then it looks like Delaney tried it on me, huh?" she asked.

"If Longworth is telling the truth."

"Did you get your telegrams?"

"Oh, yeah, I did."

"And?"

He didn't answer right away, choosing to first bite into a petit four.

"Clint?"

"Both of my contacts say Dexter St. James is fast and deadly with a gun."

"Faster than you?"

"Who knows?" he said. "Maybe."

"Well, how would you find that out?"

"Face-to-face."

"You mean you would face him without knowing first how fast he is?"

"It doesn't always come down to who's fastest, Denise," Clint said.

"Then what does it come down to?"

"It's who can hit what they're shooting at."

"And can you?"

"Every time."

"Come on," she said. "You never miss?"

"Never."

"Is that brag?"

"No, Ma'am," he said. "No brag, just fact. A man named Sonnett taught me that."

"So you're satisfied to find out how fast a man is only by facin' him?"

"Not satisfied," he said, "but often that's the only way."

"So will you walk up to him and challenge him?"

"No," Clint said, "I'll let him call the play, then give him every chance to walk away."

"But . . . why?"

"Because, despite what my reputation might be, I don't like killing people."

"I'm sorry, I didn't mean to imply—"

"Forget it," Clint said. "This cake is great. When are you going to put it on the menu?"

"I was thinkin' tomorrow?" she said. "Starting at breakfast. But I'd have to work late tonight, baking a batch of them."

"Can't you make some of them at the café?"

"I'd need to put in a good oven," she said. "Right now, all we have that we can use is a stove."

"So put in the oven."

She smiled.

"I can't afford one, at the moment."

"I see."

"So I'll be bakin' all night," she said. "If you want to come by, it'll have to be late—"

"No," he said, "after you're done, you're going to need all the rest you can get. So I'll just spend the night at my hotel." He stood up. "Thanks for the coffee and cake."

She walked him to the front door and kissed him good night.

"Remember," she said, "nice and early tomorrow."

"I'll be there . . . boss."

Chapter Twenty-Four

When Clint got back to his hotel the desk clerk waved him over frantically.

"Mr. Adams, I swear, I never said your name to anybody!" the clerk blathered.

"Take it easy," Clint said. "Tell me what's going on."

"The sheriff was here," he said. "He asked if you were in your room."

"That's okay," Clint said. "The sheriff knows who I am, and he's keeping it quiet."

"Well, he said that when you came in, I was to tell you he wants to see you."

"This late?"

The clerk shrugged.

"He said he'd be in his office, and that you should go right over," the young man said.

"Okay, then," Clint said. "I guess I'll go right over. Thanks."

"Yes, sir."

Clint left the hotel and walked over to the sheriff's office. As he entered, the man looked up from what he was doing, which was rubbing his hands together. Clint was sure it was his way of seeking some relief from the arthritis.

"Adams," he said.

"Sheriff," Clint said, "I heard you were looking for me."

"Yes, I was." Lariman stopped rubbing his hands, and because of the scent, Clint knew that the man had been rubbing something—an ointment—onto his hands. "Thanks for comin' over. Coffee?"

"Sure, thanks."

Lariman stood up, walked to the pot-bellied stove and poured two cups of coffee from the pot there. He handed one to Clint and sat. He moved pretty well, so Clint assumed the arthritis he was suffering had primarily affected his hands—and the hands were very important to a lawman.

"What's on your mind, Sheriff?"

"I'm afraid the word is gonna start getting around about who you are."

"Who'd you tell?" Clint asked.

"Nobody, but there is a man in town who recognized you," Lariman said. "That's how I knew who you were."

"And is he going to talk?" Clint asked.

"I told him not to," Lariman said, not wanting Clint to know that he had told Doc Sentry, already, "but I don't think we can count on that. So I just wanted to warn you."

Lariman actually wanted to warn Clint about Dexter St. James, but he couldn't come right out and tell him about the hired gunman. Not if he was going to continue to take Doc Sentry's money to fund his retirement, which was right around the corner. His hands were getting to the point that he was having trouble gripping his gun. He had to have enough money to retire before somebody killed him.

So he kept quiet about St. James, hoping the warning he did give Clint would be enough to keep him alive when St. James came for him.

He knew the money he was getting from Doc did not all come from the sawbones. Sentry had partners. Lariman didn't know who they were, but he suspected.

"Well," Clint said, putting his half-finished coffee on the man's desk, "thanks for the coffee, and the warning."

"Sure," Lariman said. "Just make sure you watch your back."

"I always do, Sheriff."

As Clint went out the door, he saw the older man go back to rubbing his hands.

***

Clint walked back toward his hotel, keeping alert. The street was lit by lamps, but there were plenty of shadows for somebody to hide in. But he made it back to his hotel without anybody taking a shot at him.

When he entered the lobby this time, the clerk quickly pointed. Sitting on a bench was Laura, the waitress from the Lakewood Café.

"There you are," she said, jumping to her feet.

"Here I am," Clint said, walking up to her.

"I thought you'd be coming back to the Lakewood, at some point," she said, then added, "to eat, I mean."

"I've been eating at the Well Done."

"The place I told you not to go near?" she asked, confused.

"Yeah, I guess you did warn me."

"But you're eating there anyway, instead of the Lakewood."

"Well, I pretty much have to, since I'm also the new cook, there."

She looked surprised.

"You're the steak man everybody's talkin' about?"

"That's me."

"You've cost us a little business," she said. "Not much, but a little."

"I met your boss, today," Clint said.

"Mr. Longworth?"

"Yeah," Clint answered, "when he was at the saloon, playing poker."

"He's a bit of a gambler."

"What kind of boss is he?"

"Pretty good. Hardly ever around, though. Why, did he offer you a job?"

"No, actually," Clint said. "Mr. Delaney from the Woodbury did."

"And you turned him down?"

"I did," he said. "I'm satisfied where I am."

"The Woodbury's got a huge kitchen," she told him.

"And probably too many cooks."

She shook her head.

"I don't understand," she said, "why you'd go there when I advised you not to."

"I make my own decisions, Laura," he said.

"Obviously," she said.

"Look," he said, "I've got to turn in and get an early start in the morning. Work, you know?"

"Yes, I know," she said, "work . . . at the Well Done Cafe."

"That's right."

"Well . . . I guess I'll see you around, sometime" she said, then turned around abruptly and huffed off.

Chapter Twenty-Five

Dexter St. James wasn't quite sure how to proceed.

Killing the Gunsmith would be much simpler. Just call him out in the street and gun him down. But to kill the cook named Adam, should he bushwhack him, shoot him in the back? From a rooftop? Or just walk into the café and shoot him in the kitchen?

Doc Sentry wanted Adam the cook dead, but St. James wanted to kill the Gunsmith. If he did, he'd be giving up a big pay day. Was he willing to do that? After all, he did what he did for money. But his reputation would take a big boost if he was the man who killed the Gunsmith in a fair fight.

Doc Sentry was a man of influence in this area. Did he want to get on the wrong side of the physician?

He was lingering over a beer in the Whiskey River Saloon, trying to make up his mind. He finally finished it, then left to return to Doc Sentry's house for the night. Maybe slamming his cock into Opal, the black housekeeper, from behind would relax him for a while, and his decision of which way to go would just come to him.

***

Doc Sentry entered the back room of the Woodbury Steakhouse and took a seat at the round table.

"So?" Custis Delaney said.

"St. James will do the job," Sentry told him.

"When?" Jim Longworth asked. "I don't like that he came to see me." He looked at Delaney. "Unless you sent him."

"I just went to the Well Done to take a look at him," Delaney said. "I never mentioned you."

"Take it easy," Sentry said. "Let's not turn on each other just because the Gunsmith's in town. "

Both men looked at Sentry.

"Then when is this gunman of yours going to get it done?" Sentry asked.

"Now that we know he's the Gunsmith," Sentry said, "it might take a little longer."

"Why?" Longworth asked.

"I think my gunman has a bit of a quandary on his hands."

"Explain that," Longworth said.

"He can kill Adam the cook, or he can kill the Gunsmith," Sentry said. "One of those things gives him a bigger reputation."

"And one makes him some money," Delaney said. "If he does it our way, and not his own. Where's the problem?"

"You're not concerned about your reputation, are you?" Sentry asked.

"No," Delaney said, "just about making money."

They both looked at Longworth.

"Okay, yeah, I'm a little concerned about my reputation, so I get it."

"Reputation as a restaurant owner?" Delaney asked, raising his eyebrows.

"No," Longworth said, "poker player."

"Oh."

Sentry and Delaney looked at each other.

"Hey," Longworth said, "I'm not a bad player. I just bluff too much." Something occurred to him then. "He told me that."

"Who? Adams?" Delaney asked.

"Yeah, when we talked in the Whiskey, he said I bluffed too much. I didn't know he was the Gunsmith, at that point."

"Well," Delaney said, "now that you know, maybe you can get some poker tips."

"Yeah, maybe," Longworth said.

"Better get those tips," Sentry said, "before St. James kills him."

Chapter Twenty-Six

Clint rose the next morning, looking forward to Denise bringing her baked goods into the café. In fact, he thought he would go to her house and help her carry them.

She answered the door and smiled.

"Need help?" he asked.

"Yes," she said. "I was thinking of renting a buggy to take everything over, but now that you're here, I think we could both handle it."

He followed her through the house to the kitchen, where the table was covered with various kinds of cakes and pies.

"No petit fours?"

"I thought they might be a little too fancy for the folks in this town," she said. "So I went with pies and cakes."

"That should work," he said. "Your pastries are tasty."

"I'll get them packed to go," she said. "I have some baskets."

She brought out about half a dozen wicker baskets, started filling them. They had handles, so they were able to hang the baskets from both of Denise's arms, and Clint's left. It would have been easier if he also used his right, but he had to keep it clear for his gun.

People stared at them as they walked from the house to the café. Clint had to take the key from Denise, who was balancing too many baskets to unlock the door. He unlocked it, opened it and let her go in first. Then he took a look up and down the street, and across the way, before he followed her in.

"What's wrong?" she asked.

"Somebody's watching."

"Who?"

"I don't know," he said, "yet."

***

Dexter St. James watched Clint Adams and Denise carry wicker baskets from her house to the Well Done Café. He backed into a doorway across the street just as Clint Adams turned and looked around. A man like the Gunsmith would know when he was being watched. He just didn't know who was doing the watching.

Yet.

***

"Who do you think it is?" Denise asked, as they unpacked in the kitchen.

"I don't know, but it could be somebody for hire."

"For hire?"

"A money gun, gun for hire," Clint said.

"To kill a cook?" she asked.

"Well," he said, "it seems like the word is getting around, according to Sheriff Lariman."

"The sheriff told you somebody was gunnin' for you?" she asked. "Did he say who?"

"All he said was that word was going to get around about who I am."

"From him?"

"No, he said somebody else recognized me," Clint explained. "He told them not to talk, but he didn't think they'd be able to resist."

"Okay, why would the sheriff warn you?"

"I think he's not quite finished being a lawman," Clint said.

"Even if he's takin' money from somebody in town?" she asked.

"All lawmen take a little bit," Clint said. "If he's taking more, it's because he's worried about his retirement. The arthritis in his hands is going to force him to give up his badge."

"And you support that?"

"No," Clint said, "but I do feel bad for him. And he did warn me."

"Then he should've gone one step forward and told you who he was warnin' you about."

"You're probably right."

"I have to make out today's menu and add the baked goods," she said. "I'll sit in the dining room and do it, so you can get started in here." She looked around. "I need an oven, and a bigger kitchen."

"Once people taste your desserts, it won't be long before you have the money to expand."

"Yeah, if I don't burn down first," she said, "or get forced out."

"Nobody's forcing you out," he said, "I guarantee it."

"Really?" she said. "And who's gonna enforce that guarantee if you get killed?"

"I'm not getting killed."

"You better not," she said, "because if you do, I'll never forgive you. You got that?"

"I got it."

"Make some flapjack batter," she said. "And get your steaks ready."

She turned and left the kitchen.

Chapter Twenty-Seven

By the time Denise unlocked the door for business, Clint already had steaks going on the stove, with eggs and flapjack batter ready to go. He also had some hot biscuits in a skillet, trail style. That was another thing Denise needed a real oven for.

People began to file in and, before long, all the tables were taken.

"I've never been this busy," she said. "Do you think it's because they learned who you are?"

"I hope not," he said. "Have you heard anyone say anything?"

"No," she said, "all the talk so far is about the food."

"Anybody ordering your baked goods?"

"Not for breakfast," she said. "I'll have to figure that out. Cakes and pies don't go for breakfast."

"Petit fours?" he asked.

"Maybe."

After an hour, customers had come and gone, and the tables were still full.

"This isn't gonna make my competition happy," she said.

"I'm going to guess we're hurting the Lakewood more with breakfast. Let's see if we can do the same thing tonight at supper to the Woodbury."

"I hope so," Denise said.

***

Dexter St. James was still watching from across the street, and as a second wave of customers began to leave the Well Done, his stomach began to growl. He decided it was time to go in and have another of Clint Adams' steaks.

"Hello," he said to Denise, at the door. "Remember me?"

She looked up at him and said, "Yes, I'm afraid I do. Is your head feelin' any better?"

"My head? Oh, I get it—"

"Table?" she asked, cutting him off.

"Please."

She showed him to one and said, "What can I get you?"

"Another one of those great steaks," he said. "You know, I don't usually have steak for breakfast, but with this place, it'd be a shame not to."

"I'll bring it right out."

"And coffee."

"Sure."

She walked slowly to the kitchen, so he wouldn't think he had frightened her, but her heart was pounding.

When Clint looked at her, he asked, "What's wrong?"

"He's here," she said. "He wants another steak."

"St. James?"

She nodded.

"Did he say anything else?"

"I didn't give him a chance to."

"Good for you," he said. "Okay, let's give him a good meal."

"Maybe we should poison him."

"I hope you're joking," he said, dropping a large hunk of meat into a skillet.

"Kind of."

"Poisoning a man is like shooting him in the back," Clint said.

"And you wouldn't do either?"

"No."

"I'll bring him some coffee."

"No," Clint said, "wait 'til I have his meal ready and I'll take him both. I'm sure he's here to see me, again."

"You can have him," she said. "Luckily, I still have some other customers to see to."

When Clint had St. James' steak-and-eggs ready, he carried them out to the man's table with a mug of coffee.

"Back so soon," he said, setting everything down.

"I needed one more of these good steaks," St. James said. "Especially now that I know it's bein' cooked by a legend."

"Just a cook, these days."

"Is that right?" St. James asked. "A cook wearin' a gun?"

"Well," Clint said, "somebody might complain about the food."

"I doubt that," St. James said. "This is the best steak I ever had."

"I appreciate that," Clint said. "Spread the word. And you've got to try more of Denise's baked goods."

"I will," St. James said. "But as far as spreadin' the word, I don't know how much longer I'll be in town. See, I've got a job to do, and once it's done . . . well, I'm out of town."

"A job, huh?"

"Yup."

"And just because I managed to change jobs doesn't mean you will too, huh?"

"That's right," St. James said. "My job's the same as always."

"I'll keep that in mind," Clint said.

He walked back to the kitchen secure in the knowledge that a man like Dexter St. James would not shoot him in the back.

***

Dexter St. James ate his steak-and-eggs with great gusto, feeling kind of bad that he had to kill a man who could cook like this. He enjoyed women and food more than anything in his life. Killing Clint Adams would be a damn shame, but it didn't seem to St. James that the man was the Gunsmith, anymore. It seemed as if he had truly taken on the new persona of Adam the cook.

***

"What did he say?" Denise asked.

"He was telling me how much he enjoyed my steaks," Clint said.

"That's all?"

"Actually, that's not all," Clint replied.

"Then what else did he have to say?" she asked.

"I think he was telling me," Clint said, "that he's ready to kill me."

Chapter Twenty-Eight

By the time St. James finished his meal, he was the only diner in the place. Clint wondered if that was by design. Was he going to push the issue now? He decided to push it, first.

Clint came out of the kitchen and sat across from Dexter St. James.

"Let's be honest, St. James."

"Sure."

"I know your reputation."

"I'm flattered."

"Don't be. It's not a good one. Sure, you can handle a gun, but the word is you'll do just about anything for money."

"Like what?"

"Like starting fires."

St. James didn't react to that comment. He simply finished his coffee and put the empty cup down, then wiped his mouth with his napkin.

"I think you should tell your employer that the Well Done Café is not closing down."

"Is that right?"

"Not as long as I'm the cook."

"I see," St. James said. "That's a problem they're gonna want me to take care of."

"That wouldn't be wise," Clint said.

"Why?" St. James asked. "You gonna hit me with a fryin' pan?" He chuckled.

"Just a warning, St. James."

"Well," Dexter St. James said, standing up, "let me give you some advice. Take off the apron before you try to skin your hogleg."

He dropped some money on the table and walked out. Denise came out of the kitchen, looking around carefully.

"Is he gone?"

"He's gone."

"No shootin'?"

"Not today," Clint said.

"When?"

"I don't know," Clint said. "We'll find out soon enough, though. Don't we have to get ready for lunch?"

"Yeah, we do," Denise said.

"So let's do that, and forget about Dexter St. James, for a while. What do you say?"

"I say I shoulda poisoned him," she answered, and went back into the kitchen.

***

"I want the money . . ." St. James said to Doc Sentry in the physician's office.

"To what means—"

". . . and I'm gonna do it my way," the gunman finished.

"I told you, I'd rather not have the Gunsmith killed in this town."

"Don't worry," St. James said, "I won't do it in town."

"Then where?"

"What do you care?" St. James asked. "As long as he's gone, and the Well Done closes."

"You can guarantee both?" Sentry asked.

"For the right amount of money," St. James said, "I could make this whole town disappear."

"I don't need the town to disappear," Sentry said. "Just a few men."

"A few?" St. James asked. "Somebody after the Gunsmith? Who?"

"Don't worry about that now," Sentry said, seeing the man to the door. "Just get the first part of the job done."

"I didn't even know there was a first part," St. James complained, as the door closed in his face.

Chapter Twenty-Nine

The lunch rush went smoothly, and then they cleaned up and got ready for supper.

"This is a tough business," he said, catching his breath.

"You don't have to tell me that," Denise said. "Folks are already comin' in for supper."

"We'd better get to it, then," Clint said.

One of their customers turned out to be Sheriff Lariman.

"Welcome, Sheriff," Denise said. "Steak?"

"What else?" Lariman said. "I'm ready for another one."

"Comin' up."

She went into the kitchen and said, "Steak dinner for the sheriff."

"What's he doin' here?" Clint wondered.

"He said he wants another steak."

"Or maybe he's got something else he wants to tell me," Clint suggested.

"Like what?"

"Maybe another warning," Clint said. "Okay, let me give him an extra special steak supper and see what happens."

"You see to him and I'll take care of the other customers."

"Agreed."

Clint put together a huge steak platter for the sheriff and carried it out to his table with a mug of beer.

"Well," the lawman said, when Clint put it in front of him, "that's impressive."

"Enjoy it," Clint said. "Maybe we can talk when you're done."

"Sure thing," Lariman said. "Thanks, Mr. Adams."

Clint continued to cook, while Denise carried platters out to other diners. The sheriff ate slowly, and by the time the other customers finished their meals and left, he was still there, eating a piece of pie and drinking coffee.

"Anything else?" Clint asked him, while Denise was in the kitchen.

"I thought maybe you wanted to talk to me," Lariman said.

"I thought it was the other way around," Clint said, sitting across from the lawman. "Is there something else you want to warn me about?"

"Like what?" Lariman asked, looking uncomfortable.

"Like maybe Dexter St. James?"

"Ah," Lariman said, "you've seen him?"

"Saw him, met him, talked with him," Clint said. "He's going to try to kill me. But you know that, already."

Lariman ate the last piece of his pie, put his fork down and sat back. Unconsciously, he started to rub his hands together.

"I could talk to him, try to convince him to leave town," the lawman said.

"I doubt that would work, but thanks for the offer." I just hope you don't come after me if it happens the other way around."

"St. James is pretty fast, Adams," Lariman said. "Maybe you should just leave town."

"You couldn't convince me of that any more than you could him, so don't try," Clint said.

"Okay," the lawman said, with a shrug. "So the two of you will settle it between yourselves."

"Looks that way."

The sheriff stood up, started to reach into his pocket for money.

"On the house, Sheriff," Clint said. "Come on back, anytime."

"I don't usually take free meals," Lariman said.

"That makes you a very unusual lawman, then," Clint said.

"I always have been" Lariman said. "Thanks for the meal."

***

As Sheriff Lariman left the Well Done, Dexter St. James crossed the street to fall into step next to him.

"What was that about?" he asked.

"It was about having a steak for supper."

"Really?" St. James said. "That was all?"

"What else would there be?" Lariman asked.

"Maybe you warned him?"

"About what?"

"Come on, Sheriff," St. James said. "About me. But why would you do that. We work for the same people, don't we?"

"I don't know," the lawman said. "I work for the citizens of Tenafly. Who do you work for?"

"Very funny."

Lariman stopped walking. St. James took a few more steps, then stopped and turned.

"I didn't have to warn him about you, St. James," Lariman said. "It seems you already talked to him"

"Just part of the game, Sheriff."

"You think goin' up against him is a game?"

"It sure is," St. James said, "and it's a game I'm gon-na win."

Chapter Thirty

Clint and Denise sat in the café after locking the door and ate steaks Clint had prepared.

"How'd it go with the cakes and pies?" he asked.

"People liked 'em," she said. "You might be right."

"About?"

"Turning the place into a bakery," she said. "I really like bakin' better than cookin', and when you leave, I won't have a cook, anyway."

"When I leave, you'll still have a business."

"And I'll owe that all to you," she said. "You just better come out of this alive."

"Oh, I intend to."

She put a bite of steak into her mouth and said, are you sure you wouldn't rather be a cook for the rest of your life?"

"I'm sure. "Like I said, this is a hard business."

"And being a legend is easier?"

"Let's just say I'm more used to it."

They finished eating, cleaned up and left the café.

"Where are you off to tonight?" she asked.

"I thought I might have a meal at the Woodbury Steakhouse," he said. "Take a look at the competition. And you?"

"Bakin'," she said. "I'm gonna bring in even more tomorrow."

"Then we'll need a wagon in the morning, won't we?" he asked.

"I think so."

"Okay, I'll bring one. But first I'll walk you all the way home."

***

When he walked into the Woodbury, he felt a few sets of eyes on him. A man in a suit started to walk over to greet him, but Custis Delaney was there to stop him, and came over himself.

"Returning the favor by checking out the competition?" Delaney asked.

"You said something about having a big kitchen," Clint said.

"So you came to have a look?" Delaney asked. "Fine. Right this way."

Following Delaney across the floor Clint could see how expensive the tables and chairs were, as well as the white tablecloths. When they entered the kitchen, he couldn't help but be impressed. If he really was a cook, he might have taken a job on the spot.

There were several stoves and ovens, and at least three cooks tending to them.

"Quite a set-up," Clint said.

"The ovens and stoves come from Chicago," Delaney said. "Cost a fortune to get them shipped here, but it's worth it. All I need is a cook who's as valuable."

"What about these three?" Clint asked.

"They're competent," Delaney said. "They each have their own specialty."

The aroma in the kitchen was heady, frying meats and vegetables, mostly.

"The sinks have running water," Delaney said. "Makes it easier to keep our plates and utensils clean."

"I'm impressed," Clint said.

"How about a meal?" the owner asked.

"That was my plan. Thought I'd have a steak," Clint said.

"Oh, no, no," Delaney said, "it would never be as good as yours."

"What do you suggest, then?"

"Wendell does a real good venison," Delaney said.

"I'll have that," Clint said, "and some beer."

"That's excellent!" Delaney said. "I'll show you to a table."

Delaney led Clint back to the dining room and headed for a table in the center of the room.

"Do you have something in back?" Clint asked. "Against the wall?"

"Oh, of course," Delaney said. "Stupid of me, what with your reputation and all . . . this way."

Delaney took him to a table where Clint could actually sit with his back to the wall and survey the room, and the front door.

"All right?" Delaney asked.

"Perfect."

"I'll bring the beer, and the meal as soon as it's ready," the man promised.

"Thanks."

Before long Clint was working on the beer, waiting for the meal, which came quickly. As Delaney set the plate down in front of him, the aroma came up and filled his nostrils.

"It smells great."

"And it'll taste as good as it smells," Delaney assured him. "I'll check back with you later. I have to walk around and glad hand some of the town luminaries."

Clint couldn't believe he called some of the people of Tenafly, Montana "luminaries."

Chapter Thirty-One

Delaney was right. The venison dish was very good. If the other cooks produced their own specialties as well, then the Woodbury had some fine dishes on their menu. Clint had the feeling Denise would have fit in well here with her baked goods. If she decided to change direction and give up her own place.

As the crowd began to thin out for the night Delaney came over and asked, "Mind if I sit?"

"Be my guest," Clint said. "Got any dessert?"

"We have some pie, but nothing as good as Miss Parker's," Delaney said. "Maybe now that you've seen my kitchen you can convince her to accept my offer of a job."

"You still want her if I don't come along?" Clint asked.

"Definitely," Delaney said. "I can really use someone here who can bake."

"I'll tell her what I saw in your kitchen."

"I'd appreciate that."

"That is," Clint said, "if you're not the one paying Dexter St. James to kill me and drive her out of business."

"No, not me," Delaney said. "Have you checked out Jim Longworth, at the Lakewood?"

"I've talked to him," Clint said.

"And he said he didn't hire him either, right?" Delaney asked.

"Right."

"Well, I'd believe him," Delaney said. "Jim's a gambler, but he's honest."

"But it's the two of you who would benefit from closing down the Well Done."

"Really?" Delaney sat back and spread his hands out. "You think that place can compete with this?"

"Maybe," Clint said. "Once Denise starts selling more of her desserts."

"Is that what she's going to do?"

"I don't know, maybe."

Delaney sat forward again.

"Maybe I should raise my offer," he said. "She could do some good pies, cakes and others in my ovens."

"That's true."

"Will you tell her?"

"I'll mention it. What do I owe you?"

"Nothing," Delaney said. "Let's call it professional courtesy."

"I'm not really a professional cook," Clint said.

"You could've fooled me."

***

Clint left the Woodbury and headed back to his hotel. When he entered the lobby, he looked over at the desk clerk, but this time the man just shook his head. No messages, and nobody looking for him.

When he got to his room, he took off his boots and rubbed his feet. He had been on them all day, cooking. He was used to sitting in the saddle for hours on end, but not standing in front of a stove.

He removed his shirt and washed up, then went and sat on the bed. He had met everyone involved—Delaney, Longworth and Dexter St. James. The way it looked, St. James was working for Delaney, Longworth, or maybe both. Clint decided to bounce that off Sheriff Lariman in the morning and see what he could get from the lawman.

But that would have to be after he got a good night's sleep . . .

***

The next morning his feet were still sore.

He didn't know how Denise did it, both the cooking and the waiting on tables.

After dressing and pulling on his boots, he felt a bit better. It was early—too early to go to the Well Done and open—so he decided to have breakfast alone in his hotel dining room. It was while he was there, finishing his bacon-and-eggs—that the sheriff came rushing in, looked around and then approached his table.

"Mr. Adams," he said, "I think you might want to come with me."

"What's wrong?"

"There's a fire . . ." Sheriff Lariman said . . .

***

Clint followed Lariman out and across town, but even before they got there, he saw the smoke. As they approached the Well Done Café, he saw a line of men fighting the fire with buckets of water.

"Was she inside?" Clint asked the sheriff.

"I don't know," Lariman said. "We won't know anythin' until the bucket brigade gets the fire under control."

"Damn it!" Clint said. He turned and began running toward Denise Parker's house.

Chapter Thirty-Two

When Clint reached the house, he banged his fist on the front door until it opened and Denise was standing there, frowning at him.

"What the hell—" she started, but was cut off when he grabbed her and held her to him.

"Thank God you're safe here," he said.

He released her and she stepped back.

"Well, I'm happy you're so glad to see me, but what did I do to deserve this?"

"Let's go inside," he said. "I have some bad news."

They went into the house, which smelled of fresh baked goods, and he told her about the fire.

"Oh my God," she said, tears coming to her eyes. "How bad is it?"

"It looked pretty bad," he said. "We'll know more when the bucket brigade gets it under control."

"Jesus, I should go—" She started for the door, but he stopped her short.

"There's nothing for us to do, Denise," he said.

She shook her head.

"I should've been sleepin' in the cafe," she said.

"I was thinking that's what I should've done," he said. "And whichever one of us did that would probably be burning up in there, right now."

"I guess you're right." She sat down heavily on the sofa, shoulders slumped. "Well, I guess it's over."

"Only if you let it be," he said.

"What can I do?" she asked. "I can't afford to rent another location."

"Let's just see how bad the damage is," he said. "There were a lot of men working that bucket brigade."

"Yeah," she said, "because they don't want the rest of the town to catch fire."

"Whatever the reason," he said, "they're working hard to get it under control."

Suddenly, they both smelled something burning and she jumped up.

"My pies!" she shouted and ran for the kitchen.

She was back a moment later, still shaking her head.

"Are they all right?"

"What's it matter?" she asked. "But yes, they're fine. At least my house isn't on fire." She folded her arms, her shoulders slumping once again.

"Denise," he said, "we're not going to let them beat us, are we?"

"What are we gonna do?" she asked.

"We're going to fight back."

"How?" she asked.

"I'll think of something."

***

Clint told Denise to stay in the house and keep the doors locked.

"Don't open the door to anyone but me," he said.

"What about the sheriff—"

"Nobody but me, got it?"

"I got it!"

"And keep your little gun handy."

He left the house and headed back toward the fire. When he got there, he was happy to see that the blaze was now more smoke than fire. There was a crowd of people gathered around in different groups, watching the activity. The sheriff was still standing off to one side.

"How is she?" the lawman asked.

"Safe in her house," Clint said.

"Well, that's good."

"What are you going to do about this?" Clint asked.

Lariman turned to face Clint.

"I'm gonna look into it."

"You know who set the fire, don't you?" Clint asked. "And you know who he works for. Come on, Sheriff, is it Delaney or Longworth?"

"Look—"

"Or is it both?"

Lariman looked around. There were still groups of people standing in the area, but they were looking at the smoldering building.

"You don't know what you're talking about, Adams," the lawman said.

"Then why don't you tell me?" Clint asked.

Lariman stood staring at Clint in silence.

"There's somebody else behind all this, isn't there?" Clint asked.

"Now, Adams—"

"Who is it?" Clint asked. "It's got to be a local with a lot of clout."

"Look," Lariman said, "just go and ask the right questions—but don't ask me."

Chapter Thirty-Three

Ask the right questions, the lawman said, but he wouldn't say who to ask.

Clint felt he had two choices: Custis Delaney or Jim Longworth. When he went to the Woodbury it wasn't open. Apparently, they didn't do breakfast. The Lakewood, on the other hand, was doing a brisk breakfast business, but Longworth was nowhere to be seen.

"He's probably in a poker game somewhere," a waiter said. "Or else he's sleepin' it off."

"Do you know where he lives?" Clint asked.

"I do," he said, "but we're not supposed to tell customers."

"First, I'm not a customer," he said, "and second, don't make me bring the sheriff in to get the answer."

"He has a house over on Mulberry Street. East part of town. The number is fifteen."

"Thanks."

He left and headed for the East part of town . . .

***

He found the house with the number fifteen on it and knocked on the door. He had to bang on it a second time before Jim Longworth answered, looking bleary-eyed.

"What the hell—" he started, but Clint pushed past him.

"I just thought you'd want to know your man got the job done," he said.

"What?"

"The fire," Clint said. "He got it done."

Longworth rubbed his eyes and asked, "What fire?"

"The Well Done Café," Clint said. "It finally burned down."

"I need some coffee," Longworth said. "You want some?"

He walked away and through a door, presumably to the kitchen. Clint followed him.

"So you're claiming you know nothing about the fire?" Clint asked.

"Look, I was playing poker all night," Longworth said, with a cup of coffee in his hands.

"I'm not saying you set the fire," Clint said, "I'm suggesting you had it done, by Dexter St. James."

"Dexter . . . who?"

Longworth seemed to be genuinely confused.

"Wait a minute," Longworth said. "Have you talked to Delaney?"

"Why? Is he the one who hired Dexter St. James?"

"I don't know," Longworth said. "You'll have to ask him."

"Or is there somebody else?"

Longworth froze, just for a second.

"What?" he asked.

"You heard me," Clint said. "I think there's somebody else running all of you. Somebody in this town with a lot of clout. Who is it?"

"I . . . don't know what you're talking about" Longworth said. "Look, I just got up and I can't think. Can we talk later?"

"Sure," Clint said. "Later. Just so you know, though, I'm going to find out who's behind the fire."

"I'm sure you will," Longworth said. "Is Miss Parker all right? I mean, she wasn't there when . . ."

"She was home, and she's fine," Clint said. "You tell your man, whoever it is, that I'm coming for him."

"If I knew who it was you're talking about, I'd tell him," Longworth said.

"Sure, you would," Clint said, and left the house.

Delaney was next. He hoped to find him at the Woodbury, this time.

***

"He's in his office," a waitress said, pointing. "The door in the back."

Clint walked to the door and knocked, while some of the diners looked on, curiously.

"Come in!"

He opened the door and entered. Custis Delaney rose from behind a wide, mahogany desk that must have also been imported from Chicago, like the ovens and stoves.

"Mr. Adams," he said, "come in, sit. Can I get you something?"

"Yes."

"What?"

"The man who hired Dexter St. James to burn down the Well Done Café."

Delaney appeared to be shocked.

"Burn down—has it burned down?" he asked.

"This morning," Clint said, "as if you didn't already know."

"My God, no, I didn't know," Delaney said. "And Miss Parker? Is she all right?"

"She's fine," Clint said.

"And this Dexter St. James," Delaney went on. "You believe he's the one who burned it down? Have you talked to the sheriff?"

"I have," Clint said. "He says he's going to look into it, but I suspect he already knows who set it, and who hired it done."

"Well, then he should act."

"But he won't," Clint said. "We all know that. He's at the end of his trail, and it wouldn't be in his best interest."

"What are you saying?" Delaney asked. "You think I was behind this?"

"You, Longworth, or both," Clint said. "But I think there's another man behind the two of you, and that's who I want."

Delaney seemed to be weighing his options. Maybe he was actually considering giving the man up.

"Mr. Adams," he finally said, "I assure you—"

"Don't assure me of anything, Delaney," Clint said, "just tell that man I'm coming for him, so he better send St. James to take his shot. But if he doesn't get the job done, I'll have you all."

"Adams—"

"I've talked to Longworth, and now you," Clint said. "Burning down the café was despicable. I'm warning you all that I'm coming—and not as a cook!"

Clint turned and stalked out.

Chapter Thirty-Four

Clint went back to the fire, saw that most of the on-lookers had left, as had the bucket brigade. There was still smoke, but no flame. The sheriff was inside.

Although the café was still standing, it wasn't going to be doing any business for a long time. The inside was scorched, black, all the tables and chairs reduced to kindling, the walls black and damaged.

"How's the kitchen?" Clint asked, as he entered.

Lariman turned and looked at him.

"I ain't looked yet, but I think the fire started in there," he said.

"I'll take a look," Clint said.

He was almost through the door when some of the roof suddenly, collapsed. He jumped back just in time.

"Whoa," Lariman said, "you okay?"

"Yeah," Clint said, waving his hand in front of his face to dispel the smoke. "I think you're right. It must have started in there."

"Could've been an accident," Lariman said. "The stove?"

"That's not likely," Clint said. "We make sure everything is doused before we leave. Besides, you know for a fact this wasn't an accident."

"Mr. Adams—"

"Never mind," Clint said. "*I* know for a fact it wasn't an accident."

"Did you talk to Longworth and Delaney?" the sheriff asked.

"I did," Clint said. "They both claim not to know anything about it."

"And you don't believe them."

"I don't believe anything they—or you—tell me," Clint said.

"Okay," Lariman said, "I guess I'm done, here."

"Done?"

"Looks to me like it started in the kitchen," Lariman said. "I say it was accidental."

The lawman turned and left before Clint could say anything.

***

"He's callin' it an accident?" Denise said, in disbelief.

"That's what he said," Clint said.

"And you're sure it wasn't, right?"

"Right. You and I know we didn't leave the stove on when we left."

"Right," she agreed.

141

"So no accident," Clint said. "That means that Dexter St. James probably set it."

"But he's a professional gunman, right?" she asked. "Why set a fire?"

"Probably because he was told to."

"By who?" she asked.

"That's what I'm trying to find out," he said. "I talked to Delaney and Longworth, but I think there's somebody telling them what to do."

"Like who?"

"I don't know," he said. "And what bothers me is that Longworth knows, Delaney knows, and the sheriff knows."

"So it's like everybody knows but us, huh?"

"Yeah."

They were sitting in her living room, unsure of where to go now that there was no café to open.

"Okay," she said, finally, standing up. "I have to go look."

"At the damage? Why?"

"Because seeing what happened is better than what I'm imagining . . . don't you think?"

Before he could answer she was on her way to the door.

Chapter Thirty-Five

Clint walked Denise to the site of the fire, her former Well Done Café. There was nobody else around, so he was the only one who saw her start to cry.

"Denise—"

"I'm fine," she said. "I just wanna go inside."

"Okay."

They went in together and she stood in the center of the debris and looked around.

"Do I want to see the kitchen?" she asked.

"You don't," he answered.

"Jesus," she said, "what a mess."

"Could be worse," he offered.

"How?"

"There are still walls, most of a roof," he said. "With some work, you could be up and running again in a month."

"Do you think I could actually get somebody from this town to do the work for me?" she asked. "And how do I live until then?"

"I have an idea about that."

***

Jim Longworth entered Doc Sentry's office.

"I'll be with you in a minute," Sentry said. "I have a patient."

"I'll wait."

Sentry went into his examining room, came out minutes later with an older woman.

"If the pain comes back, you come and see me right away, Alma, you hear?"

"I hear, Doctor," she said.

He showed her out the door, then turned to face Sentry.

"So he did it," Longworth said.

"Who did what?"

"Your man, St. James," Longworth said. "He burned down the Well Done Café."

"Did he?" Sentry asked. "When?"

"Last night, or this morning, I guess," Longworth said. "The bucket brigade put it out this morning."

"That's too bad," Sentry said. "And the lady? Was she inside?"

"No, she was home," Longworth said, "but Clint Adams came to see me this morning"

"About what?"

"About you."

That surprised Sentry.

"He mentioned me?"

"No," Longwood said, "but he said that there was somebody else behind me and Delaney. And that somebody else hired St. James."

"And you told him it was me?"

"I told him to check with Delaney," Longworth said. "So if somebody gave you up, it was Custis."

"I'll have to talk to him about it," Sentry said. "Anything else?"

"Yes," Longworth said, "Adams said you better have St. James go after him, because he's coming for you."

Sentry frowned.

"Then I guess I better have him do just that."

***

Clint took Denise back to her house and told her to stay there.

"What are you gonna do?" she asked.

"Try and find some answers."

"Where?"

"I don't know," he said, heading for the door. "I'll just keep looking and asking questions."

***

In Clint's experience, bartenders and hotel desk clerks knew more about what was happening in a town than anybody. So he decided to start with the clerk in his hotel who, up to now, had been very cooperative.

"No messages, Mr. Adams," the young man said, as Clint approached him.

"That's fine," Clint said. "But maybe you can help me with a question."

"I'll sure try."

"Who's the biggest man in town?"

"You mean . . . tallest?" the clerk asked.

"No," Clint said, "I mean the richest, or the most influential."

"Well, I'd think the fellas who own the Woodbury and the Lakewood were pretty rich," he said. "And probably the mayor."

"But who has more to say about what goes on in Tenafly?" Clint asked.

"Well, gee," the clerk said, "I'd think the mayor and the sheriff."

Clint wasn't getting what he wanted from the young man, so he said, "Okay, thanks."

He left the hotel and headed for the Whiskey River Saloon.

Chapter Thirty-Six

He had never found out the bartender's name in the Whiskey, but the man was obviously more seasoned than the hotel desk clerk, and the Whiskey seemed to be a place most of the townspeople frequented.

It was early when he walked in, though, so the gaming tables were covered and there was only one girl working the floor. The bartender was in place, wiping down the bar with a rag.

"A little early," the bartender said. "Beer or coffee?"

"I'll take coffee, thanks."

The bartender put a mug on the bar.

"What can I do for you?" he asked. "You look like a man with a problem."

"I am," Clint said. "I need to know whose thumb everybody in this town is under."

"Well," the man said, "I own this place and I ain't under anybody's thumb, but I know what you mean. The two biggest businesses in town are the Woodbury and the Lakewood."

"Delaney and Longworth," Clint said.

"Right. Now Longworth, he's a bit more interested in poker than he is in his restaurant."

"Then why does he own it—oh, wait, don't tell me he won it in a poker game?"

"Exactly," the bartender said. "It's doin' well, in spite of him. But he's gonna drive it into the ground, if somebody doesn't win it off of him, first."

"So he doesn't have a lot of influence in town," Clint said.

"No, not him."

"What about Delaney?"

"That's possible, but I don't think so," the bartender said. "He's real involved in running his restaurant, and doesn't even like the competition from the Lakewood, even though they both have their own regulars."

"But they didn't like what was going on at the Well Done, right?"

"Right, especially not when you started cookin' there," the man said. "And then findin' out who you really was . . . well, that didn't make 'em happy."

"Once word got out, what were people saying?" Clint asked.

"Well, a lot were sayin' you cooked a great steak," the bartender said, "but most were sayin' that gal hired you for your gun."

"So then somebody brought a money gun into town named Dexter St. James," Clint said. "Who would he be working for? Come on, who has the most influence in Tenafly?"

"Well," the man said, rubbing his jaw, "I could give you a few names . . ."

". . . but you've got one, don't you? What's your name?"

"I'm Harlan Gauge, Mr. Adams."

"Well, come on, Harlan," Clint said, "I get the feeling you know everybody in town and everything that's going on. In fact, you might be the guy I'm looking for."

Gauge smiled.

"I ain't that smart, Mr. Adams," he said. "The feller you want is the one who's been in this town the longest, the one all the little people love, but all the business owners are afraid of."

"Harlan," Clint said, "I get the feeling I should've come to you the first day I got here."

"You're probably right about that," Gauge said.

"So what's the name?"

"Now wait a minute," Gauge said. "Not everybody in town's gonna be happy if you take this feller down. You might be bitin' off more than you can chew. You could end up with most of the town against ya."

"I'm not worried about that," Clint said. "I want the man who burned down the Well Done, and I want the man behind him."

"You figurin' St. James did the burnin'?"

"I am."

"You gonna call 'im on it?"

"I am," Clint said, again.

"Then maybe you can get him to tell you who hired him," Gauge suggested.

"I doubt it. If he gives up his employer, there's not much chance of him ever getting hired again."

"Not much chance of that if you kill 'im, either."

"I've talked with the man, already," Clint said. "He's pretty confident."

"Then where's the harm in tellin' you who hired him if he figures he can kill you."

"That's a good point," Clint said, "but I'd still like to hear your suggestion."

"I gotta live in this town, Mr. Adams," Gauge said.

"If the name you give me is the right one," Clint said, "I'll owe you, and nobody will ever hear that I got it from you."

Gauge looked around. There were only two customers in the place, and they were seated at tables with whiskey bottles in front of them. The only other person was the saloon girl, and she wasn't paying any attention to them.

"So, I'd be holding a marker from the Gunsmith, huh?" Gauge said.

"That's right," Clint said. "And you can call it in any time."

"Well then," Gauge said, "if I was you, I'd have a talk with Doc Sentry."

Chapter Thirty-Seven

"Is that just a name, or is he the town doctor?"

"The town doctor," Gauge said. "That's why I'm sayin' you might not be so popular in this town if you take him down."

"I'll risk it," Clint said. "Tell me about him."

"Well, everybody figures he was just born with the town," Gauge said, "been here his whole life. Most of the businessmen seem to owe him."

"You don't?"

"I bought this place on my own just a few years ago," Gauge said.

"And Longworth won his," Clint said. "Does Sentry own him?"

"Seems to, though I don't know why."

"And Delaney?"

"Came to town about ten years ago, wanted to open the Woodbury. I heard he didn't have the funds, and then suddenly, he did."

"Doc Sentry?"

"He's real quiet about it," Gauge said, "but Doc's the richest man in town."

"How rich?"

"Pretty damn rich," Gauge said, "but you wouldn't know it from the way he lives."

"Why would a rich man be worried about a small café and its owner?" Clint asked.

"I couldn't answer that for sure," Gauge said.

"Take a guess."

"Maybe," the bartender said, "it's because she's not under his thumb, like the rest of the town is."

"And neither are you, right?"

"Right."

"Thanks, Gauge. Oh, one more thing."

"Yeah?"

"Where can I find Doc Sentry?"

***

Clint found Doc Sentry's office, with a shingle outside that said: DR. G. SENTRY, M.D.

He entered the office, found it empty, but heard voices from the next room. He sat down to wait. Finally, the door opened and a tall, older man with white hair came out, leading a younger man with his arm in a sling.

"Now do what I tell you this time, Ed," the doctor said. "Don't use that arm for a week. Let somebody else do some of the work, for a change."

"Sure thing, Doc," the man said, and left.

The doctor turned and looked at Clint, who stood up.

"You look pretty healthy," the doctor said.

"Which probably doesn't make you very happy."

"Sorry?"

"Clint Adams, Doc. I think we have some things to talk about."

"Really? Like what, for instance?"

"Fire, for one," Clint said. "Dexter St. James, for another."

"I don't think I know anything about either of those things, Mr. Adams."

"What if I told you that word has it you're the man who brought St. James to Tenafly?"

"I'd wonder who would tell you a bold-faced lie like that, Mr. Adams."

"I've also been told nobody has more influence in this town than you."

"I've been lucky to serve this town for many years," Doc Sentry said. "If I've influenced the people here, I'm pleased."

Clint studied the man. He had to be in his mid-sixties and seemed to be a very gentle man. Could the bartender, Gauge, have given Clint the doctor's name for another reason? Something personal, maybe? Or was he just guessing wrong?

"Anything else I can do for you, Mr. Adams?"

"Yes," Clint said, "tell St. James to come on and get it over with. And just before I kill him, he'll give you up."

"Well, if I knew this St. James, I'd warn him to stay away from the Gunsmith," Sentry said. "That'd be a whole lot healthier for him, wouldn't it?"

"It would, yeah," Clint said.

"But I don't," Sentry said. "Sorry."

Clint studied the man for a few beats, hoping to unnerve him, but the doctor didn't seem to have any nerves.

"Anything else?" Sentry asked. "I've got some more patients coming in any minute."

"No, nothing else," Clint said. "I just wanted you to know I'm onto you."

"Then you should probably go to the sheriff," Sentry said.

"Who you have firmly under your thumb," Clint said. "Yeah, I've already talked to him."

"He didn't give you my name," Sentry said. "I know Sheriff Lariman too long to believe that."

"No, he didn't," Clint said. "He's too worried about his retirement for that."

"The sheriff should enjoy his retirement," Sentry said. "He's earned it."

"I'll tell him you said so."

Chapter Thirty-Eight

Clint needed somebody who was in the know to turn on Doc Sentry. His choices were Delaney, Longworth or Sheriff Lariman. He decided on the lawman.

He found Lariman in his office, sitting behind his desk, looking miserable.

"I talked with Doc Sentry," Clint said, sitting in front of the desk.

"You did?" Lariman asked. "You feelin' sick?"

"Kind of, after the fire," Clint said.

"How did the lady take it?"

"Not well," Clint said. "But I promised I was going to find out who set it and make them pay."

"Them?"

"The man who set the fire, and the man who hired him to do it."

"Did you talk to Delaney and Longworth?" the sheriff asked.

"I did," Clint said. "They weren't very helpful."

"So what was this about Doc Sentry?"

"I asked around to find out who had the most influence in town," Clint said. "Came up with Doc Sentry."

Lariman sat back, wincing. Clint didn't know if it was because of what he said, or pain.

"So what did Doc have to say?"

"Nothing," Clint said. "He doesn't know anything, he doesn't know anybody who'd burn down Denise's business, but he knows everybody in town."

"Well, yeah," Lariman said, "he's treated most of the people who live around here. They love him."

"And what about the people he was in business with? How did they feel about him?"

"In business?"

"Come on, Sheriff," Clint said. "A man with Doc's money's got to be investing it. Is he part owner of the Woodbury? The Lakewood? Both?"

"I wouldn't know, Mr. Adams."

"I bet you've been in this town as long as Doc. If anyone knows his business, it's you."

Lariman winced again. Then he sat up, gripped his chest, and slumped from the chair.

"Oh hell!" Clint swore.

He quickly checked the man to make sure he was still breathing, and then ran to get the doctor.

***

"Heart attack," Doc Sentry said.

Sentry had run to the sheriff's office pretty fast for a man his age, grabbing a few men off the street along the way. They carried Lariman back to his office, with Clint following them. He sat and waited while Sentry treated the lawman.

"How is he?" Clint asked.

"Not good," Sentry said. "Right now he can't move."

"It's too dangerous to move him?" Clint asked.

"No," Sentry said, "I mean he can't move. He's paralyzed. And he can't talk, so why don't you tell me what you did to him?"

"I didn't do anything to him," Clint said. "We were just talking. He grabbed his chest and fell out of his chair. He was wincing from pain, and I thought it was his arthritis."

"No, it was his heart," Sentry said.

"I'm sorry about that."

"So if you were looking to get something incriminating from him," Sentry said, "you're going to have to look somewhere else."

"Thanks," Clint said. "I think I'll do that."

"Good luck," Sentry said. "I have to get back to my patient."

"Good luck to you, too, Doc."

***

With Sheriff Lariman out of commission Clint had to go back to thinking about Delaney and Longworth. It was a matter of figuring out which one he could turn.

Or he could simply go after Dexter St. James.

He decided to take a look around town, stick his head in the saloons, and see if he could locate St. James.

He tried the Whiskey River first, but there was no sign of him there. After stopping at three other saloons with no luck, he wondered what was going on? St. James certainly wasn't following him. He would have known if he was. Was he in hiding after the fire? And if so, where?

He stopped at several hotels, without any luck, which he expected. Then something occurred to him. Whoever hired him was probably boarding him, as well. And if that was Doc Sentry, then all he needed to do was find out where the doctor lived.

He headed for his hotel.

***

As usual, the young clerk was on duty.

"Doc Sentry?" the clerk said. "Sure, I can tell you where he lives. But his office is right down—"

"That's okay," Clint said. "I've been to his office. But I need to know where his house is."

"I'll give you directions . . ."

Chapter Thirty-Nine

Following the clerk's directions Clint found his way to Doc Sentry's house. It was in a part of town that had homes resembling those in the South, two stories with white pillars in front.

He approached the front door, was about to knock, but then thought better of it. If Dexter St. James was inside, that would be warning him.

So instead, he got down off the porch and walked around the side of the house. The curtains were drawn on all the windows. He continued to the back, saw a barn there with a small corral. He found the barn door unlocked and entered. Inside was a buggy, and three horses. One was obviously for the buggy, probably eight years old and sway backed. The other two were saddle mounts, one much fitter than the other. He was willing to bet that was Dexter St. James' horse.

There were saddles, but no saddlebags. He decided it was time to go ahead and knock on the door.

He made his way to the front of the house, up onto the porch again and knocked on the door. A young black woman answered and stared at him without speaking.

"I know Doc Sentry's not home," he said, "but I need to speak with Dexter St. James."

"I don't know who dat is," she said.

"I think you do," Clint said. "Tell him I'm here, or I'll just come in and find him."

"Who you be?" she asked.

"Clint Adams."

She frowned.

"You bad man."

"That's right," he said, "and so's St. James. We're two of a kind. So tell him I'm here."

"No," she said, firmly.

"It's okay," St. James called out from inside. "Bring Mr. Adams in, Opal."

She glared at Clint and said, "You come in."

"Thank you."

She led him through an entry hall into a sitting room furnished with plush, expensive furniture. St. James was sitting on the sofa, holding a snifter of what looked like brandy.

"You want a drink?" he asked Clint. "We'll have to be quick. Doc'll be home soon, and he don't like anybody drinkin' his brandy."

"No thanks," Clint said. "I'm not interested in brandy."

"It's okay, Opal," St. James said, looking past Clint. "Wait for me upstairs."

"I t'ink dis a bad man," Opal said, and walked away.

"Does she know you're a bad man?" Clint asked.

"I ain't been bad to her."

"What is she to Sentry?"

"His housekeeper and cook."

"Does he know about the two of you?" Clint asked.

"He does."

"That's funny," Clint said. "He told me he never heard of you."

"I'm not surprised."

Clint noticed that while St. James lounged on the couch, he still wore his sidearm. He understood that perfectly.

"Siddown and relax," St. James said, "I ain't gonna draw down on you in this house."

"I believe you, but I'll stand."

"What brings you here?"

"A fire," Clint said.

St. James frowned.

"What fire? That door? I didn't mean nothin' by that. It was just . . . a reminder. I knew it wouldn't burn the place down."

"No, not that fire," Clint said. "The one that did burn the place down this morning."

"What?"

"That was you, right?"

162

"No!" St. James snapped. "Look, I don't set fires, not normally. I let . . . somebody talk me into settin' fire to that door. But I wouldn't burn the whole place down." Then he looked alarmed. "The lady wasn't inside, was she?"

"No, she was home."

"And it happened this mornin', you said?"

"That's right."

"Talk to Opal," St. James said, "she'll tell ya I was here."

"I'm sure she will."

"No, she's a good girl," the gunman said. "She won't lie to you."

"But you are working for Doc Sentry, right?" Clint asked.

"Doc's an old friend," St. James said, "he's givin' me a place to stay."

"Riiiiight."

"Look," St. James said, "you and me are gonna go head-to-head, but not today, and not with fire."

Clint couldn't help but believe the man.

"Okay," Clint said, "then I'm back to square one. Who burned the café down if not you?"

"Beats me," St. James said, "but if I was you, I'd leave before Doc gets home. He's my host, and if he tells me to draw on you while you're in his house—"

"I get it," Clint said. "Look, I'm going to find out who burned the Well Done down, and then you and I are going to talk again."

"I can't wait," St. James said, and sipped his brandy.

Chapter Forty

If Dexter St. James didn't burn down the Well Done Café then there was a new player in town. Or an old one who Clint was just finding out about.

He managed to get away from Doc Sentry's house before the sawbones returned home. The fact that St. James was in the doctor's house, sleeping with his housekeeper, convinced Clint that Sentry had brought St. James to town to get rid of the Well Done. Discovering that the Gunsmith was in town was a bonus for the man. But Clint believed that setting fires was not St. James' style. In fact, he seemed embarrassed to admit he had set fire to the door.

By the time Clint reached the center of town, he was once again convinced he had to look closer at Delaney and Longworth. Who else but the owners of the two restaurants would want the third restaurant in town burned down? And there was still a chance Doc Sentry was in it with them.

Clint decided to stop by Doc Sentry's and check on the sheriff.

***

"He's recovering," Sentry said, as he let Clint in. "That's why I'm still here. I've got to keep an eye on him. But the way he's going it looks like it wasn't a heart attack, after all, just some spasms. He should be back on his feet soon."

"Do you have any idea who will take over his job until then?" Clint asked. "Does he have any deputies?"

"No," Sentry said. "Replacing him is not going to be up to me."

Clint wasn't so sure that was true.

He decided not to tell Sentry he had been to his house. Let St. James tell him that, if he wanted to.

"Okay, thanks, Doc," Clint said.

"If you want to talk anymore," Sentry said, "I'll probably be here all night, trying to keep my friend alive."

Clint nodded and left. The man seemed to truly be concerned with the welfare of Sheriff Lariman. He was, after all, a doctor—perhaps first and foremost.

As Clint walked back to Denise's house, he wondered if the sheriff had been about to tell him something before he suffered his attack? But if Doc Sentry managed to pull the lawman through the night and save his life, Clint doubted the man would ever say anything against the sawbones.

He knocked on Denise's door and she looked relieved when she answered and saw it was him. She also looked extremely worn out.

"Come in," she said. "I was worried. What have you been doin'?"

Once inside they sat and he told her about his visit to Doc Sentry's house, and how he came to be there. He also told her about his talk with St. James.

"Wait a minute," she said. "I'm confused. Doc Sentry? What's he got to do with anythin'? He's a kindly old sawbones."

"That's what he wants people to think," Clint said. "And the fact that St. James is his house guest proves that he's got other things going on."

"Like burnin' down my place?"

"That's just it," Clint said. "St. James told me he didn't do it."

"And you believed him?"

"I did, yeah."

"Great."

"But I still think Doc Sentry had something to do with it," Clint said. "Maybe along with Delaney and Longworth."

"So what are you gonna do?"

"The same thing I've been doing," he said. "Ask questions. I just wanted to make sure you were all right."

"Oh, I'm just dandy," she said. "I'm baking, can you believe that?"

He sniffed the air and said, "Yeah, I can believe it."

"I don't know what I'm gonna do with it all, but there you are. That's what I'm doin'."

"I've got an idea what you can do with it," he said.

"Yeah, what?"

"Just give me time. I'll be back."

***

"You want me to what?" Delaney asked.

Clint had gone back to the Woodbury Steakhouse and found Delaney still in his office.

"I want you to buy some baked goods from Denise Parker," Clint said.

"How much?" Delaney asked.

"Everything," Clint said. "There's nothing she can do with them, and she doesn't want to throw all of it out. You've tasted her baking, you know she's good."

"We're coming to the end of our supper rush," Delaney said.

"I'm sure you can store it all someplace and sell everything tomorrow," Clint said.

Delaney studied Clint from behind his desk.

"Are you authorized to sell these things to me?" he asked. "Negotiate a price?"

"I am."

"Okay," Custis Delaney said, "let's talk."

Chapter Forty-One

"You did what?" Denise asked.

"I got Delaney to buy your baked goods for the Woodbury," Clint said, again.

They were sitting in Denise's kitchen, surrounded by cakes, pies and petit fours.

"Why'd you do that?" she asked.

"It gets you some income, keeps you from having to throw all of this away, and it gives Delaney an investment in you."

"Investment?"

"Once his customers taste your baked goods, they're going to want more," he said. "Delaney won't do anything to drive you out of town. He'll try to hire you."

"I don't wanna work for him—"

"Make him pay you a lot," Clint said. "Save your money, and then reopen your own shop."

"So that means Delaney will be financing my new place," she said.

"Without knowing it."

She thought a moment, then said, "That's brilliant. But first we have to get that gunman to leave me alone."

"I'll make sure he and Doc Sentry don't bother you."

***

After sex that night, Opal asked St. James, "Are you going to kill dat bad mon?"

"I am, yes," he said. "I was hopin' to take him out of town and do it, but now it looks like I'll just have to do it in the street."

"Why do you not jus' shoot him in de back?"

"Because that ain't no way for a man like the Gunsmith to die, Opal," St. James said. "Men like him and me, we're gonna die from a bullet in the front."

"I don't understand," she said, rubbing her hand over his bare chest. "I do not want you to die."

"Well, I don't wanna die, either," he said. "But we're gonna see how it goes."

"But you—"

"Time for you to shut up, Opal," he said, pushing her head down between his legs, "and open wide . . .

***

For the moment there was no law in Tenafly. For that reason, Clint felt he had to stay close to Denise.

"Are you going back to your hotel tonight?" Denise asked Clint.

"No," he said, and explained. "If I'm right and Dexter St. James didn't set that fire, then there's somebody else out there we have to worry about. So I thought I'd spend the night here with you."

"Or we could go to your hotel," she suggested.

"I considered that, too. But if we did that," he said, "I'd be afraid we'd come back here tomorrow and find burnt out rubble."

"Okay then," she said, "we'll stay here."

"But we've got one more thing to do tonight."

"What's that?" Denise asked.

At that moment there was a knock at the door.

"I'll get that," Clint said.

He opened the door to two men who had parked a wagon out front.

"Come inside," he told them.

"What's going on—" Denise started, as they followed Clint in.

"They're from the Woodbury, here to pick up your baked goods," Clint said. "They can keep them fresh overnight. You want to show them where it all is?"

Denise showed the two men into the kitchen, and then the four of them carried everything out and loaded it onto the wagon in the fading light.

"Here you go," one of the men said to Denise, handing her an envelope. "Good-night, Miss."

The two men climbed up onto the wagon and drove it off as Clint and Denise went back into the house. Once inside, Denise looked in the envelope and found the money Clint had negotiated for.

"Oh, my God," she said.

"That should hold you for a while," Clint told her. "And he said if you bake more, he'll take more."

"I don't know what to say," she said. "Can you be so sure I'm not actually takin' money from the man who burned down my place?"

"I'm not dead sure," he admitted, "but I don't think he would've done this if he had. And I've seen his kitchen. You could bake up a storm with those ovens."

"This is unbelievable, Clint," she said. She rushed him, put her arms around him and hugged tightly.

"Now," he said, "did you keep anything for us to have with some coffee?"

Chapter Forty-Two

Clint woke the next morning with Denise lying on her left side, facing away from him. They were both naked after a vigorous night. He wondered if getting her to sell her baked goods to the Woodbury might solve her problem. Maybe she wouldn't even need to rebuild the café. If that worked, she would be safe, and he could leave Tenafly. He was sure Eclipse was getting restless in the livery stable.

He rose without waking her, dressed and went down to the kitchen to make coffee. His life was starting to feel a little too domesticated these days, and he needed to get back out on the trail.

But making sure Denise was safe was only part of the problem. He was going to have to deal with Dexter St. James.

***

When Dexter St. James came downstairs that morning, Doc Sentry was waiting at the foot of the staircase.

"Today's the day, St. James," he said.

"For what, Doc?"

"I want Adams taken care of."

"But you said you didn't want it done in town," St. James said, "and that it should look like the cook—"

"That's not the case, anymore," Sentry said. "Everyone in town knows who he is."

"So Adam the cook is gone?" St. James asked.

"Yes, damn it!" Sentry shouted. "Everyone knows he's Clint Adams, the Gunsmith. So do it any way you want, anywhere, but get it done."

"You got it, Doc," St. James said, then added, "right after breakfast."

***

Clint had coffee on the table by the time Denise came downstairs, wearing a robe. He also had some of her cakes alongside the coffee.

"Breakfast is served," he said, "that is, unless you prefer eggs?"

"This is wonderful," she assured him.

He held her chair out, then sat down across the table from her.

"Did you sleep well?" he asked.

"Well, enough," she said, smiling impishly "when you let me."

"I thought we'd go over to the Woodbury, this morning," he said.

"What for?"

"So you could take a look at their kitchen, and their ovens," he answered. "We can also see how your cakes are selling."

"Mr. Adams, are you tryin' to take my mind off the fire?" she asked.

"Well . . . yeah," he said. "I sure as hell don't want you to be sitting at home thinking about it. That won't do any good."

"Clint," she said, "as soon as I have enough money, I'll get my café rebuilt. I want to have my own place."

"I realize that," Clint said. "As we just confirmed, I'm trying to take your mind off things."

"And by things," she asked, "you mean you and this Dexter St. James?"

"That's not for you to worry about, Denise," Clint told her.

"Nevertheless," she said, "I am worried. When is . . . that . . . gonna happen?"

"If I'm any judge of the situation," he said, "probably today."

"Oh God," Denise said, and bit into a cake covered with vanilla frosting.

***

After breakfast St. James sat back to enjoy one last cup of coffee while Opal cleared the table. Knowing what she looked like beneath the long dress made the watching all the more enjoyable.

At the head of the table sat Doc Sentry, who had finished his breakfast and coffee.

"I have to get to my office," he announced, standing. "I have patients." He glared at St. James. "And you have some business."

"Relax, Doc," St. James said. "I already told you, I'll handle it."

"You'd better," the doctor said. "I want this to be all over by the time I come home tonight."

St. James gave the man a mock salute, and the doctor strode from the room and stormed out of the house.

St. James once again thought about Opal without her dress on. He stood and went into the kitchen to see what he could do about that.

Chapter Forty-Three

As Clint and Denise entered the Woodbury, Custis Delaney approached them with his arms spread wide, and a smile on his face.

"Already a hit," he announced.

"That's good news," Clint said.

Denise looked around, saw several of the tables chowing down on her cakes.

"Have you come to see our ovens?" Delaney asked.

"That's what Clint wants me to do," she said, "so, yes."

"Then let me take you to the kitchen."

"Lead the way, Mr. Delaney," Denise said. "Let's see what you've got."

"This way," he said.

Denise looked at Clint. "Coming?"

Clint turned and followed her into the kitchen. When he got there, Denise was already leaning over one of the ovens. When she turned her head and looked at him, her eyes were shining.

"Have you seen these ovens?" she asked.

"I have."

"My God," she said.

"I told her she can try them out any time," Delaney said.

Did he want to entice her into working for him, or was this to make up for burning her place down?

"It's an impressive setup," Clint said.

Delaney took Denise to the back of the kitchen to show her where and how they stored food. Clint stood there looking around, while the cooks and wait staff stared at him curiously.

When Denise and the restaurant owner came back, Clint said to him, "I guess your staff knows who I am."

"Mr. Adams," Delaney said, the whole town knows who you are."

"That doesn't sound good," Denise said.

"That's the way life is, for the Gunsmith," Delaney told her, then looked at Clint and asked, "Right?"

"Pretty much," Clint said.

"Well," Denise said to Delaney, "thanks for showin' me around."

"Any time," Delaney said. "And my offer still stands. You can start working here whenever you like."

"I'll keep it in mind."

"I'll be right out," Clint said.

"Sure."

She went through the kitchen doors to the dining room to wait for him.

"What's on your mind?" Delaney asked as one waiter passed them leaving the kitchen.

"She's not going to work for you," Clint said, "unless she's convinced you didn't have her place burned down."

"I didn't."

"You don't have to convince me," Clint said. "Just her."

"But if I convince you," Delaney said, "you can talk to her."

"Then all you have to do is convince me, I guess," Clint said.

"Then I've got two words for you," Delaney said.

"What are they?" Clint asked.

Delaney looked around, lowered his voice and said, "Doc Sentry."

***

First St. James checked Clint Adams' hotel. Not finding him there he went to the Well Done café. He had heard that it burned to the ground, but he thought he might find Adams and the woman going through the rubble.

Not finding them there, he decided to simply walk around town and, when he ran into Adams, get the job done. There didn't seem to be any point in dragging it out any longer.

***

"What was that about?" Denise asked, when they had stepped outside the Woodbury.

"I think he wanted a favor."

"What favor?"

"To convince you to work for him."

"What did you tell him?" she asked, as they started to walk.

"That you'd never do it unless you were sure he wasn't responsible for your place burning down."

"You didn't tell him I wouldn't do it, at all?"

"No," Clint said, "it's not my place to close doors for you. You'll have to tell him that, yourself. Unless you decide to go ahead and do what we discussed."

"Which was?"

"Let him pay to rebuild your place."

"Well," she said, "those ovens *are* inviting. But first, do you really think he had nothin' to do with the fire?"

"I don't know for sure, but I don't think so."

"Longworth, then?"

"No," Clint said, "I'm pretty sure it's Doc Sentry. I thought so after I spoke with him, and now Delaney mentioned his name."

"What did he say?"

"Just that," Clint said. "He gave me a look and said, 'Doc Sentry.'"

"The town doctor?" Denise said. "Why would he want to drive me out?"

"According to what I've heard, he's the richest man in town, with pieces of many businesses. I assume he's part owner of either the Woodbury or the Lakewood. Maybe both."

"How are you gonna find out for sure?"

"I'll ask somebody."

"Who?"

"Adams!"

Clint turned, saw Dexter St. James striding toward them.

"Him," he said.

Chapter Forty-Four

As Dexter St. James reached them Clint used his left hand to push Denise off to one side.

"Adams," St. James said.

"St. James. What can I do for you?"

"I think you know," St. James said. "It's time."

"Before we do this," Clint said, "I want to know who hired you?"

"Why?"

"I'm just curious. Who wants me killed bad enough to hire somebody of your caliber."

St. James laughed.

"You playin' on my ego, Adams?" he asked.

"Maybe I am," Clint said. "But come on, if you're going to kill me, there's no harm in telling who you're working for. Is there?"

"Maybe not," St. James said, "but it ain't somethin' I usually talk about."

"You don't have to talk about it," Clint said. "Just tell me if you're working for Doc Sentry."

"Why Doc?" St. James asked.

"You're staying in his house."

"We could just be friends, couldn't we?" St. James asked, with a shrug.

"He's rich and you're for hire," Clint said. "That doesn't exactly speak of friendship."

"You been for hire for years—"

"My gun has never been for hire," Clint corrected him.

"That ain't what your reputation says, Adams."

"You shouldn't believe everything you hear, St. James," Clint told him. "Reputations are a lot of horse-shit."

"Is that right?" St. James asked. "So you ain't as fast as they say you are—or were?"

"There's only one way for you to find that out," Clint replied.

"Well," St. James said, "that's what I'm here to do, find out."

"You've got a chance right now to mount up and ride out," Clint said, "and keep on living."

"Wow, is that the line you use on everybody to try to scare them away?"

"No," Clint said, "it's just good advice. Mount up and ride out."

"Save your good advice for somebody who needs it, Gunsmith," Dexter St. James said. "Do you wanna do it here, or in the street?"

"Your choice," Clint said, "Just tell me you're working for Doc Sentry."

"Of course I'm workin' for Doc Sentry," St. James said. "Who else in this town would be able to afford me?"

"I'm just thinking Doc Sentry might have some partners—"

"Look," St. James said, "I told you what you wanted to know. Now let's get this done."

"One more thing."

Exasperated, St. James asked, "What now?"

Clint pointed at Denise.

"Tell the lady who burned down her place."

St. James looked at Denise, who was staring at him, warily.

"Well, Ma'am," he said, "I don't rightly know who did it, but I can tell ya I didn't."

"Am I supposed to believe a killer?" she asked him.

St. James looked at Clint and said, "He believes me."

"Do you?" Denise asked Clint.

"Yeah, I do."

St. James stepped into the street.

"Let's do this, Adams," he said.

Clint started to step into the street, but Denise grabbed his arm.

"Clint!"

"I'll be right back, Denise," he said.

"And if you're not?"

"Go to work for Delaney," he said. "That'd probably be the best place for you."

She nodded and released his arm.

"Adams!" St. James called.

"Don't be in such a hurry to die, St. James," Clint said, stepping into the street.

Chapter Forty-Five

Sheriff Lariman looked up as the door to his office swung open and a man ran in. He rolled his eyes, because he had only just returned to his office after his supposed "heart attack," which tuned out to be "spasms."

"What's wrong, Jasper?" he asked.

"Over on Lincoln Street, Sheriff," Jasper said. "The Gunsmith's in the street with some feller."

Dexter St. James, Lariman thought. The money gun was making his move.

"What're ya gonna do, Sheriff?"

"Don't you worry about it, Jasper," Lariman said. He tossed the town drunk a coin. "Go and have a drink."

"Thanks, Sheriff!"

Jasper left, and Lariman stood up, grabbed his hat, moving none too fast . . .

***

Clint moved to the center of the street as a crowd began to build on both sides, to watch.

Denise remained in her doorway, from where she could see everything. She didn't know what she would do if St. James killed Clint. Run? Hide? Or take Clint's advice and work for Delaney.

Clint studied St. James, looking for a tell. A "tell" was usually something you saw at a poker table, that told when your opponent had a good hand. In this case, Clint was looking for something that would give him an edge, if it turned out his ability with a gun simply wasn't enough. The time was coming when he'd go up against somebody faster, better than him. But he was looking to put that time off a little longer.

St. James was standing stock still, not giving anything away. That was probably why he was still alive. So this would come down to who was fastest, plain and simple.

St. James was a talker, but not now. The talking was all done.

***

Lariman made it to the end of the street before the action took place. He stopped where he was. He was close enough to see who was who. Suddenly, both men moved incredibly fast, but there was only one shot, and then one fell to the ground.

He started walking toward them . . .

***

188

St. James was very fast. His gun had cleared leather and was coming up when Clint fired a round into his chest. Clint walked to him to make sure he was dead, then stood there and waited for the sheriff to reach him as he ejected the spent shell from his gun and replaced it. At the same time, Denise stepped into the street and hurried to him.

"Thank God!" she breathed.

"Mr. Adams," Lariman said, as he reached them.

"Sheriff," Clint said. "Welcome back. What'd Doc say?"

"I'll live." He looked down at St. James, bent over to check him, then stood back up. "Dead."

"Yep."

"Did he tell you who he was workin' for?"

"He did."

"Why?"

"That's what you're asking me?" Clint asked. "Why not who?"

"I wanna know why he'd tell you who he was workin' for, and why you'd believe him."

"He told me because he thought he was going to kill me," Clint said. "And I believed him for the same reason. He had no reason to lie."

"And what about the fire?"

"He said he didn't set it."

"And you believed him?" Lariman asked.

"Yeah, I did."

Lariman took a deep breath.

"All right," he said, "let's have it. Who hired him?"

"Doc Sentry."

"Shit!" Lariman swore.

"Are you gonna arrest him?" Denise asked.

"It's not that simple, Miss," the lawman told her.

"Why not?" she asked.

"Because," Clint said, before the sheriff could speak, "he's a rich man, with influence in this town."

"Just because he's rich doesn't mean he can hire killers," Denise said. "And if this man didn't burn down my place, then Doc Sentry probably hired somebody else to do that. And I could've been inside!"

"I'll talk to Doc," Lariman said.

"Talk to him?" Denise repeated. "That's all?"

"That's all I can do, for now," Lariman said. "And only after I get this body off the street."

He walked over to the crowd on one side of the street and started pointing out men to "volunteer" to move the body.

"Come on," Clint said to Denise.

"Where?"

"To do some talking of our own, while the sheriff's busy."

.

Chapter Forty-Six

The door was opened by the black housekeeper, Opal, who just glared at them.

"Is Doc home?" Clint asked.

"Is he dead?" she asked.

"Who, Doc?"

"No," she said, "Mr. St. James. Is he dead?"

"Yes, he is."

She scowled.

"Did you kill him?" she asked.

"Yes, I did," he said. "He didn't leave me any choice. It was either kill him, or let him kill me."

"You should have let him, den," the woman said.

"That's stupid," Denise said.

The woman turned her scowl on Denise.

"He's dead because of you," she said.

"That's not true," Clint said. "He's dead because Doc Sentry hired him, and because he wanted to better his reputation."

"The doctor is in his office," the woman said, and slammed the door.

"Wow," Denise said, "she's pretty upset."

"Well, while St. James was staying here, he and the housekeeper became . . . close."

"Ah . . ." Denise said, understanding. "So now what?"

"Let's go see the doctor at his office," Clint said.

***

As they approached the office, the door opened and the sheriff stepped out.

"Looks like you made the right choice," Clint said. "We went to his house."

"I knew the doc would be here," he said.

"And where are you off to now that you talked with him?" Clint asked. "Do you have your orders?"

"I don't know what you mean," Lariman said, "but I'm goin' to his house to arrest Opal, his housekeeper."

"The housekeeper? Why?"

"Apparently, she set the fire."

"Is that what the doctor told you?"

"It is."

"Why would she do that?" Denise asked.

"She thought that would save St. James from havin' to go up against the Gunsmith," Lariman said. "But that didn't work. Now she'll have to pay."

"So St. James is dead, Opal will be in jail, and nothing happens to the doctor?" Clint asked.

"And the lady will be safe from any harm," Lariman said, nodding toward Denise. "I've got Doc's word."

"You mind if we go in and talk to him?" Clint asked.

"I don't mind," Lariman said, "as long as you don't interfere with my job."

"I'd never do that, Sheriff."

Lariman walked away, while Clint and Denise entered the doctor's office.

"Mr. Adams," Doc Sentry said, "the sheriff just left—"

"Yes, we saw him," Clint said. "Seems you sent him to your house to arrest your housekeeper."

"Yes, poor Opal," he said. "I don't know what she saw in Dexter St. James, but her feelings caused her to make a bad decision." Sentry looked at Denise. "I'm sorry about your café, Miss Parker."

"I'm sorry about your hired killer, Doc," she replied.

"He was not my killer, Miss Parker," Sentry said. "Just my houseguest. Whatever else he did, he did on his own."

"Not according to him," Clint said. "Before he died, he said you hired him."

"He was lying, of course."

"I don't think so," Clint said.

"Well," Doc Sentry said, "I guess it's his word against mine, then."

"Maybe not."

"Meaning?"

194

"You just sent the sheriff to arrest Opal," Clint said. "You don't think that's going to make her mad enough to talk?"

Sentry frowned.

"But don't worry," Clint said. "Even if she does talk, I doubt the sheriff would take action against you, Doc. So here's what I'm proposing. From here on in you leave this lady alone. Whether or not she reopens her place, or gets another job, you leave her alone. If I hear that you've gone after her again, I'll come right back here and blow your head off. You got that?"

"Yes, I've got it, but—"

"No buts!" Clint snapped. "Don't try to claim you weren't behind this whole thing. And I don't even care why. You probably just didn't like the idea of a business in this town that you don't have a piece of. Maybe it hurt your ego. I don't care, because if it doesn't stop here and now, if you—or anyone—harms her, I'll do more than hurt your ego."

Clint didn't wait for a comment. He took Denise's arm and directed her through the door.

"Did you mean that?" she asked, when they got outside.

"Every word."

"You'll come back and kill him if he bothers me?"

"Yes. The man hired a killer to get rid of me. If he bothers you, I'll give him what he deserves."

"What if he sends someone else after you?" she asked.

"He already bought the best and it didn't work."

"So you think he'll leave me alone, now?"

"Yes."

"And what about that poor black girl?"

"She probably did set the fire, Denise," Clint said. "She broke the law."

"So what do you think I should do?"

"I don't know," he said. "Work at the Woodbury until you have enough money to reopen. Or just work at the Woodbury from now on."

"And you're still convinced that Mr. Delaney didn't have anythin' to do with burnin' down my place?"

"I am."

"And what about the other man, Longworth, who owns the Lakewood?"

"I think both those men may be in partnership with Doc Sentry. They may know what he was up to, but I don't think they made any move to harm you."

"And if they are partners?"

"Sentry will tell them what I said," Clint said.

"That's why you told him if he or anyone bothers me . . ."

"Right," Clint said, "him or his partners."

196

"So does this mean you're leavin' town?"

"Yes."

"Right away?"

"Well," he said, "not this very minute. Why, what did you have in mind?"

"A way for me to say thank you, and goodbye," she said, taking his left arm.

"And does it involve baking?" he asked.

"Maybe," she said, "after . . ."

Coming January 27, 2020

THE GUNSMITH
455
Brotherly Love

**For more information
click here:** www.SpeakingVolumes.us

On Sale Now!

THE GUNSMITH
453

**For more information
visit:** www.SpeakingVolumes.us

On Sale Now!

THE GUNSMITH *series*
Books 430 – 452

For more information
visit: www.SpeakingVolumes.us

On Sale Now!

Lady Gunsmith *series*
Books 1-8

For more information
visit: